Christmas Voices

John Callas

Library of Congress Copyright Card Number: (Reference) 1-5779061471

14th Street Publishing
Santa Monica, CA

ISBN-10: 1976022827
ISBN-13: 978-1976022821

Printed in the United States of America

ACKNOWLEDGMENTS

Editor:

Karl Monger

www.karlmonger.com

Cover Design:

Daniel Martin Literary

www.dmels.com

DEDICATION

For Mom, Dad,
My loving and supportive family
Linda, Stephan, Nicholas,
and
To all who believe in the magic of Christmas.

FOREWORD

Since 1990, my wife Linda, and I have developed a tradition of building a Christmas Village out of Department 56 collectable pieces. The village collection started under our Christmas tree with a few select pieces. Each year the collection has grown. It now sits on a platform that is 5 1/2 feet wide and 22 feet long.

With over 800 trees, hand carved mountains, gondolas, skiers, trains, special lighting that we created and built for the village, and Charles Dickens porcelain houses, we have become known to be one of the world's leading collectors at this scale. The village is built every other year as it takes 6 weeks to construct. - And no two years look alike.

Christmas Voices was inspired by this collection and the love of the spirit of Christmas. It is a modern day blend of *A Christmas Carol* and *It's A Wonderful Life*. A story that will warm the hearts of children and adults, while rekindling the belief in miracles.

Please visit: facebook.com/Christmas Voices

Chapter One

This cold, crisp night brings the Christmas holiday that much closer for the Daily family. Living on a farm isn't easy and never has been. The conditions, even worse than last year, are about as tough as any farm owner could be expected to handle. The Daily's old farmhouse sits in the middle of a field surrounded by beautiful shade trees whose barren branches are frozen in place until the spring thaw. Dried stalks from last year's harvest jut out from beneath the snow. The temperature has fallen to 18 degrees as animals nestle together trying to keep warm. Snow sparkles as smoke rises from the chimney. The dead of winter has announced itself throughout the fields. Even the man-made lake that Christopher Daily stocks with trout in the summer is a solid mass of ice. The farmhouse is decorated with a single strand of multi-colored Christmas lights.

Inside the farmhouse is a modest fireplace that, was handcrafted by Christopher to help keep the house warm and cozy. Sitting in the corner, precariously resting on a makeshift table, is an old black and white television. Its rabbit ears are wrapped with aluminum foil struggling, mostly in vain, to achieve better reception from the three channels that are available in the area. On a small table fashioned from an old tree trunk sits a radio playing "Let It Snow."

Seven-year-old John Daily is a kind-hearted kid who loves his family and doesn't mind the simple life of living on a farm. John is a good student who is taunted by the other children for his worn-out clothing and his family's impoverished lifestyle. One of his favorite things is to snuggle in bed with his mom and dad and listen to them tell stories about Christmas. He always imagines himself talking to Santa and working with the elves to create presents. His fantasy is that all kids will get everything they want for Christmas.

John tried playing sports but in the end decided

that working on the farm provided enough exercise for anyone. Instead of playing sports during recess, John can be found in the library. After all, what better place than the school library to satisfy his voracious appetite for reading?

During the Christmas season, John spends endless hours in the den playing with his family's Dickens Christmas Village. It's a tradition that has been handed down since the time of his father's father and will one day be handed down to John. The village sits on a platform located next to a Christmas tree modestly decorated with mostly handmade ornaments. Strings of popcorn circle the tree, photos in handmade frames dangle between branches, and paper cutouts of Santa and his reindeer accent the colorful lights.

The Christmas village is made up of porcelain houses, carved mountains, village figurines, a farm, a church, and a ski area, all covered in plastic snow as a train circles through and around the mountains. Smoke rises from a porcelain house while John speaks with the figurine people that populate the village. These imaginary friends comprise one of John's only solaces.

"Billy, are you getting everything from Santa that you asked for?" he says in his normal voice.

He answers as Billy in a different voice. "No, my

folks are poor."

John responds, "So are mine, but I think I am getting a bicycle this year."

Billy replies, "You are so lucky. I asked for ice skates. Can you ask Santa for me?"

As John carries on, other imaginary voices from the village chime in with their requests.

"Can you help our church with food for the hungry?"

"Our house is going to be taken away unless we pay the bank."

"My son needs an operation that we can't afford."

John gingerly picks up one villager after another, listening to the plight of each one. He takes time to hear about their problems then softly replaces each of them on the village platform in the exact spot they were before. His eye catches one in particular. He lifts it up, and examines it closely. It's a figurine of a beggar. Like John, his clothes are worn, and he wears a look of desperation on his face. There is an unspoken connection of sympathy with this figurine that piques his curiosity. He knows how painful it feels to be poor and in need. It is a pain that comes every year at this time when the presents are few even though the love is plentiful.

He speaks to the beggar. "How did you arrive at

this place in your life?"

The reply is simple. "It's a long story, but I could use some help."

After putting the beggar back down, he stands smiling over the village and proudly announces that he promises to help each of them no matter what it takes. It is a promise that fills his entire being and one whose full meaning he will someday discover.

In the kitchen is John's mother, Mary, an attractive woman in her late thirties. She is a proud woman who makes the most of what little she has without uttering a single complaint. As long as she has her family she can make-do with dire circumstances. She always dresses nicely, though her wardrobe reveals the hard reality of wear and tear with no money to fix them. The soft lace barely holds together and the dress displays signs of repeated mending. Her shoes are clean, although they sport cracks that suggest their age. She is at the sink peeling potatoes that have been stockpiled since harvest time. Her husband, Christopher, is in his early forties. He sits at the kitchen table wearing a pair of overalls contemplating a stack of bills. His hands are the hands of a worker, with cracks and swollen knuckles. He is a strong man who knows what is entailed by a hard day's work. Having little money, he has scraped together only the bare necessities to run the farm and keep the lights on in the house. As Christmas nears, the holiday spirit is thwarted by a poor harvest and lack of sufficient funds to make the holiday special for his wife and son. He hems and sighs deeply with each bill he reviews. He knows there isn't enough money to pay them all, and with the poor harvest that's staring him in the face, things could not look worse.

"It just never ends."

Mary continues to peel the potatoes. "How bad is it?"

Mary waits patiently for a response but none comes. She stops peeling potatoes and looks at him. His face is drawn. She knows the pressure this time of year brings, and knowing how much Christopher loves his son, it makes the holidays less than merry. Her spirits are always high and are what Christopher draws his strength from when things are at their worst. Mary pulls out a chair from the table and takes a seat.

"What are our options?"

Christopher pauses, then looks up at her, unable to find a way to disguise the facts.

"Well, we have a little money in our savings, but that won't last long. We could always..."

He can't bring himself to say it. Mary gives him a

tender look, her eyes caring and loving. She has been his strength when he was down just as he has been her shoulder when she needed to cry. They are a perfectly matched couple, but at the moment they sit on bad times.

"Christopher, if it comes to selling our livestock to survive, then we have no choice. We can always buy more when things improve. Or we sell the farm."

Christopher crumbles a bill in frustration.

"That's the problem. All we're doing is surviving. What about John? How do we provide for him and give him an education? Or even a decent start in life?"

Mary slips out of her chair and sits on his lap. "Christopher, look at me. We have given him a wonderful loving family life and, by building the village each year, a priceless Christmas tradition. Those will stay with him always. Money can't buy everything he needs. You are an amazing father to him, and that will get him through any challenges life throws at him. He's a very smart and motivated kid. I am sure he will be fine."

They are unaware that John is standing quietly in the hallway next to the kitchen and inadvertently overhears every word they say. John returns to the family room and goes over to the village, puts his hands on his hips, leans in, and speaks with authority.

"Okay, villagers, listen up. I, John Daily, do hereby promise that I will become very rich and powerful and give you everything you want, no matter what it takes. No one will ever be poor or need anything ever again."

John stands basking in the realization of his commitment to the people of the Christmas village. Mary and Christopher walk into the living room and join him. Mary goes over to John.

"Who are you talking to?"

John smiles at his mom. "My friends in the village."

Christopher puts his arm around John's shoulder.

"You really love this village, don't you?"

John hugs his dad tightly.

"I wouldn't know what to do without the village and my friends. They mean the world to me."

Mary's eyes grow misty as she looks at her son. She is as proud a mother who has ever loved her child. She is confident John will find himself and get ahead in life. She prays that he will not have to struggle like they have and wants, like every mother, to have grandchildren.

"Mom, do you think the people in the village hear me when I talk to them?" John asks.

She is not sure how to respond. "What do you think, honey?"

John looks at his parents and giggles. "Of course they do. They answer me, don't they?"

It is a cherished moment for the family and carries with it the spirit of Christmas. Mary thinks about a way to mark this special moment. It comes quickly to her.

"How about some freshly baked cookies and some warm milk?"

John's face lights up as bright as the Christmas tree. "YES, PLEASE!"

She looks at John and Christopher. "Then it is settled. I'll see you both in the kitchen. But only one or two cookies before dinner."

Mary goes off to the kitchen.

"Dad, do you think God listens to our prayers like the people of the village listen to me?"

Christopher looks at the village, then at his son. He has always given John excellent advice and something to think about. He has been exemplary in guiding John to make his own decisions, and this moment is no exception.

"You know, son, that is a great question. I guess what it really boils down to is a matter of belief. If you believe in something strongly enough, then I suppose it becomes real."

John ponders his dad's words.

"So, if the people of the village believe I can help them, then they will get their wish?"

Christopher isn't sure how to answer the question.

"Umm, what do you think they want?"

A slight smirk lifts the corners of John's mouth. "Well, I know one of them wants a pair of ice skates. Another wants to live in a fancy house. One actually is a mean old man who makes their lives miserable."

Christopher's eyes furl. "Which one is that one?"

"You know, Dad. Scrooge."

"Oh yeah, almost forgot about him."

John eyes his dad conspiratorially.

"You know, Dad, one of them told me he really, really, REALLY wants a bicycle for Christmas."

Christopher knows the game is afoot and doesn't want to let on that he probably cannot afford to get him a bicycle for Christmas. Christopher always manages to turn a bad situation into a tolerable one for the benefit of his only son.

"Oh, he did, did he? And what did you tell him?"

John struggles to keep a straight face.

"I told him we were poor but that I MIGHT get one from Santa. Do you think Santa will bring me one for

Christmas?"

Christopher's heart is wrenched by the word "poor," but he hides his feelings. He never makes money the subject of a discussion with his son. Although Christopher lacks a formal education, he is creative in finding ways to relate to John without upsetting him. In the summer, when all the kids are having ice cream treats and Christopher and Mary can't afford it, Christopher turns it into a game by suggesting that apples are far more delicious than ice cream because they are loaded with sugar. John never refuses the apple and quickly forgets about ice cream.

"Well, Santa has a lot of kids wanting a lot of toys. But let's hope he can build you one. Okay?"

John hugs his father. "I love you and mom more than anything in the whole wide world."

"And I love you more than anything in the whole wide world, too."

The father-son moment is one that Christopher treasures, along with Mary giving them the most wonderful gift of all--a loving family—even though she has had to sacrifice so much in the process.

The smell of freshly baked cookies wafts into the family room as Mary calls from the kitchen.

"They're ready."

Christopher challenges John.

"Race you to the kitchen."

Before Christopher can even finish his sentence John is already sprinting for the kitchen... and the most delicious cookies on the planet.

Christopher smiles. "Cheater."

John giggles as he runs. He quickly takes his seat at the table and waits with anticipation for his mom's mouth-watering homemade chocolate chip cookies. They are soft and gooey, and the chocolate dribbles when John pulls them into two halves for dunking. Just the way John likes them. Munching them down at Santa's-sleigh speed followed by gulps of milk, John is reminded that dinner will be ready soon and he is only allowed two cookies. His mom wipes the milk moustache off John's face and tells him to go wash up.

Before they begin eating, they hold hands, bow their heads, as Christopher thanks God for the food on the table, the love they share, the blessings they enjoy, and for guidance in making the right decisions. They say Amen in unison. The dinner is simple but nutritious. Most of the food was grown during the spring/summer season along with fresh meat proportioned to get them through the winter.

After dinner and with a full belly, John gets ready for bed. With his Christmas pajamas on, he looks into the bathroom mirror and daydreams about the coming hours and the arrival of Santa. In his mind he hears the hoof beats of reindeer on the roof. He imagines Santa getting out of his sleigh, grabbing the largest toy-filled bag, slinging it over his shoulder, and climbing into the chimney. Inside the house Santa's red coat emerges from the chimney and he enters the family room with his huge bag of toys. Then magically, and at lightning speed, Santa pulls out the dream bicycle that he has had his eye on for months. After placing the bike under the tree, Santa gobbles the cookies, swallows the milk, and with a HO HO HO is vaporized up the chimney. On the rooftop John hears the reindeer's hoofs as they begin pulling Santa's sleigh. Then with a whoosh, Santa is off at incredible speed to deliver the rest of the presents before dawn, when children everywhere will wake to the joys and surprises left for them the night before Christmas.

John spits out his toothpaste, rinses his hands and mouth, shuts off the water, dries his face, and heads to his bedroom. Once in bed, he is tucked in by his mother, who kisses him goodnight. Christopher strokes his son's hair and kisses him.

"Goodnight, son. Sleep well."

"Goodnight, Dad. Goodnight, Mom."

"Don't forget to say your prayers," Mary says as she turns off the overhead light, leaving only a small nightlight on. Christopher gently closes the door.

John thinks about what his dad said about believing in something so strongly that it comes to pass. He tosses and turns knowing Christmas is just around the corner and thinks about how much he wants that bike. He rolls over and closes his eyes hoping to fall into a delightful sleep, filled with fantastic dreams of sugar plum fairies and all the trimmings he has come to associate with Christmas. He fluffs his pillow and lays his head back down, but it is no use. He rolls onto his back and stares up at the ceiling. He thinks about his village friends. He wants to help each and every one of them because he knows what it is like to not have much.

Clouds begin covering the sky and moon, and John's room falls into ever-deeper darkness. His thoughts continue to challenge him until he gets out of bed and goes over to the window. As the last cloud obscures the heavens, he falls on his knees, gazes into the night sky, and folds his hands together.

"God, if you can hear me, please put in a good word for me with Santa. Dad says Santa has a lot of kids asking for lots of presents at Christmas. I only want one thing, and I know you know what that is."

He stops to make sure God is listening and has heard his request.

"My dad says if you believe strongly enough, anything is possible. How can I tell if I believe in something strongly enough? Okay, so here goes."

John slowly closes his eyes. "I believe that it will snow. I believe it with all my might."

He becomes silent so the words can float out the window and up to heaven. After a short time, a gentle wind starts to blow. He smiles knowing that God has heard his prayers and is sending him a message. He opens one eye and looks out the window for signs of snow, but there is nothing except the wind. He closes his eyes, squeezing them   tighter than a drummer drumming. Again he opens one eye and scans the cloud-covered sky for a sign – nothing. He closes his eye again.

"I believe. My dad told me if I believe it will happen, and Dad is never wrong."

His face begins to relax as he opens one eye again. He searches the sky - Nothing. Then from the darkness a single snowflake hits the glass.

"SNOW!" It is followed by another flake. "SNOW. SNOW." A few more hit the window. John's other eye pops open. "SNOW. SNOW. SNOW. SNOW. SNOW." Snow is falling heavily against his window. John jumps up and runs in a circle with his arms stretched toward heaven.

"I did it. I BELIEVED IT AND IT HAPPENED!!! I will have everything I want and more because I BELIEVE."

Chapter Two

Christopher drives through town sinking into a depressed state of mind as he contemplates whether to sell the farm animals or the farm itself. He feels on the verge of exploding, knowing the desperate situation his family faces. He is a good man who loves his family, and he now feels he has let down those who mean the most to him. He prays every night in search of answers but so far none have come. His faith is unwavering and he never succumbs to the temptation to give up hope. Looking around, he knows they are staring at a long hard winter and a threadbare Christmas for his son. He hears John's voice echoing in his mind... *And one boy really really really wants a bicycle for Christmas.* How can he afford such a gift when it's a struggle to keep his family fed, the bills are piled to the ceiling, and last year's harvest barely produced? He looks at his watch to make sure he will be home in time for dinner.

Christopher continues through town, passing stores filled with Christmas shoppers. A few friends wave as he passes by. He returns the gesture with a smile, all the while feeling torn up inside. Although the town is small, it is well decorated, with the Christmas spirit on full display. As he drives, his eyes land on one store that is not decorated, Miller's Pawn Shop. Christopher considers whether or not he has anything of value to pawn. Maybe the attic holds something nestled in a corner? All his thinking produces nothing that is worthwhile. Frustrated, he slams his fist against the steering wheel. Christopher is not a violent man. His reaction is one of frustration and disappointment. Plagued by the thought that he cannot provide properly for his family, he feels less than what a man should feel. Fortunately, Mary has been a beacon of strength and unconditional love throughout their marriage. She never makes mention of their situation and always finds the positive in everything. Every morning she has a smile, a kiss that says I love you, and hot coffee when he comes into the kitchen ready to face another day. Each day she reminds Christopher and John that there is plenty for them to be thankful for. He looks at his watch again and decides to pull over and see what it might be worth. Maybe he can get enough for his watch to give John his dream bicycle and a Merry Christmas.

Christopher parks, turns off the engine, and sits staring at the pawn shop. He is a very proud man, and he is about to do the hardest thing he has ever done in his life. His thoughts start to get the best of him. *What if people find out that I did this? Will they wonder if my family is more destitute than they suspect? How will Mary be able to look the other women in the community in the eye and still hold her head up? How might the kids in school treat John? Will they tease him about how poor he is? Will they say bad things about his father?* He knows his son loves him, but a child can only endure so much. Christopher takes several deep breaths to calm down, gets out of his truck, and enters the pawn shop, where he is greeted warmly.

"Morning, Mr. Daily."

Christopher hangs his head in embarrassment.

"Morning, Mr. Miller."

Mr. Miller senses something is not quite right.

"And what brings you in today?"

Christopher looks Mr. Miller straight in the eye, and even though Mr. Miller knows what is about to happen he never lets on.

"Well, you see, Mr. Miller, I have this here watch that I don't really need anymore. So I was wondering what you might pay for it?"

Christopher takes off his watch and hands it over. Mr. Miller takes one look at the watch and knows it is worth about $30.00 tops. He makes a show of examining it again and then looks at Christopher. He sees the torment in his eyes.

"Now this here is a mighty fine watch. Are you sure ya wanna sell her?"

Christopher's heart beats fast and hard. His stomach rises and falls, but he holds it together. He doesn't want to sell his watch, but there doesn't seem to be any other solution.

"Yes, Mr. Miller, I'm sure. I really don't need it anymore, and there is something that means more to me than this watch."

Mr. Miller studies Christopher a little more, then replies, "Well, seeing as you don't need it anymore and it's a good watch, what say I give you $40.00 for it?"

Christopher is torn. One side of him wants to scream Halleluiah and the other side wants to shout his anguish at having to pawn his watch.

"Thank you, Mr. Miller. I accept your kind offer."

Mr. Miller opens the register and hands Christopher two twenty-dollar bills. Christopher takes the watch off and hesitates before handing it to Mr. Miller.

"Would it be all right if we keep this transaction between you and me, please?"

Mr. Miller knows how hard this must be for Christopher.

"Of course we can. Our little secret. And if you ever change your mind, you can come back and pay exactly what you received. Deal?"

Christopher feels relieved. "Deal. And thank you."

Mr. Miller smiles. "Merry Christmas."

"Merry Christmas, Mr. Miller, and God bless you." Christopher opens his empty wallet and places the cash inside. He takes his leave, knowing in his heart he will never see his watch again. Still, it will be well worth the sacrifice to see John's face light up on Christmas morning.

Inside the truck Christopher smiles for the first time in months. There is a sense of relief, even though he knows it is temporary. All he cares about is the look on John's face on Christmas morning. It's an image that will stay with him the rest of his life. He starts the truck, puts it into gear, backs out of the parking space, and heads toward the department store to buy John the one present he asked Santa to bring. Christopher's smile broadens, feeling like one of the Christmas shoppers filled with the spirit of Christmas.

Christopher walks into the busy department store. The shoppers, dressed in holiday clothes, remind Christopher of his lack of money; he grows self-conscious in his overalls and worn-out winter jacket. His mind is trying to grab hold of everyone around him shopping at fever pitch, grabbing, shoving, and pushing their way through to the next 'On Sale' item. He beholds this mass of confusion and simply shakes his head. Looking up, he sees a sign pointing him toward the toy department. Navigating through the crowd and up two flights of escalators, he finds the toy department in the rear of the store. Once again he maneuvers through the beehive of milling shoppers. He finally reaches the toy department and sees rows of bicycles lined along the back wall.

Christopher pulls the magazine page that John gave him out of his pocket. It shows the bike his son wants Santa to bring to him. On the glossy paper John has written his height so Santa gets the right size for him. Christopher thinks to himself, *That boy doesn't miss a thing.* John is in fact very detailed and methodical in everything he does, including his chores. He takes enormous pride in getting it right the first time and not wasting a single minute to accomplish the goal he has set for himself. John is also good at saving money. He has a piggy bank that he puts all his loose change in, occasionally shaking it to see how full it has gotten.

A salesman sees Christopher holding the magazine page and approaches him.

"Good day, sir. Are you looking for a bicycle?"

Christopher looks up. "Um, yes. This is the one I am looking for." He hands the page to the salesperson.

"Ah, that is one of the finest bikes we sell. Please come this way and I will show you. Who's the lucky kid?"

"My son."

Christopher follows the salesman to the section where John's soon-to-be-Santa-delivered Christmas gift is sitting.

"Here we are. Isn't she a beauty? I see you have written on the page your son's height.

"Actually he wrote it. He is very detailed."

"I see. Well this model will certainly make him happy."

"Yes, it will. May I ask how much the bike costs?"

"Well, as I said, this is one of our finer bikes so

price isn't really that important compared to the happiness of your son on Christmas morning, now is it? Just think of all the joy he'll have riding his brand new bike down the street, parading in front of all his friends while you and the Mrs. stand proudly watching. It is a memory that will last a lifetime."

Christopher just stares at the salesperson, wondering what language this guy is speaking. All he asked for was the price, not a rundown for emotional blackmail.

"Well, where I come from a simple question deserves a simple answer."

"Including tax, it comes to $39.00. How will you be paying for it?"

His tone has changed to something that is more to Christopher's liking.

Christopher pulls out his wallet, knowing precisely how much money is inside. He removes the bills and hands them to the salesman, who scurries off. Christopher touches the bicycle and smiles, imagining the joy on John's face when he sees it resting next to the Christmas tree. The salesman returns with Christopher's change.

"Here you are, sir. Your change is one dollar. I am sure your son will be very happy with his bike."

Christopher inquires, "Would it be all right to pick

it up tomorrow evening before you close?"

"Of course. But keep in mind we close early because it is Christmas Eve."

Christopher turns and heads back toward the escalator, steadying himself to face the swarming shoppers on his way out of the store. He opens his wallet and places the bill inside.

"Well, it's just you and me, dollar."

Sunday arrives, and the Daily family puts on their best clothing. It shows wear and tear, but they do the best they can with what they have. Mary makes sure that Christopher and John's shoes are polished so the scuff marks don't show too much. She dresses in a bonnet and wraps a shawl around her shoulders. The only jewelry she dons is from the costume section of the local store. She never feels inferior to the other women but often hears their gossip about her family's financial situation. She refuses to give in to embarrassment or defend herself with them. She is the quintessential embodiment of pride and dignity. She holds her head high knowing her family is a family of love, and that is all she has ever wanted.

The Daily family heads to church in their beat up pickup truck. They never miss Sunday mass and always put something in the basket as a gesture of gratitude for what they have. They enjoy listening to

Father James's sermons. He always manages to give voice to what the congregation needs to hear that week. Christopher listens hoping to hear something that can help with his situation. Although he doesn't get any answers, his faith never lets him doubt they are there. Mary listens for spiritual reassurance, and John listens to learn the lesson at hand.

Volunteers go from pew to pew collecting donations for the church. Christopher looks at Mary, who smiles at him. As the collection plate approaches, Christopher opens his wallet and stares at the dollar bill. Two churchgoers are glaring at him with scorn on their faces. They are the neighborhood gossip queens and the source of 90% of local rumors. Both are widowed and spend their free time swapping juicy stories, some of which they make up simply to outdo the other. Mary overhears their snide remarks. She is not bothered by what they say, knowing who they are and how they deal with the community.

Mrs. Basler whispers to Mrs. Highland. "I hear they are about to lose everything and may have to sell their livestock."

"That's still no excuse to not give to the church."

Mary turns to the two of them and smiles. They turn away, embarrassed. Christopher looks at John then takes the dollar from his wallet and drops it into the collection plate. Mary takes Christopher's hand and squeezes it to assure him that he did the right thing. She believes that positive thinking will always bring positive results, something she hopes she has instilled in John.

Father James approaches the end of his sermon.

"We must always remember the joy of giving and the peace of forgiving. There is nothing more valuable than to reach out to our neighbors and help them when they are in need. Then and only then will your salvation be complete."

The congregation replies, "Amen!"

Father James leaves the pulpit and heads up the aisle to say goodbye to his flock as they leave. One by one he shakes their hands, wishing them God's grace. The Daily family is next in line.

"God be with you and your family," says Father James.

Christopher leans in close to Father James.

"Father, may we have a private word with you in your office, please?"

Father James nods. "Of course, Christopher. I will meet you there in a few minutes."

Father James enters his office. Christopher and Mary stand up to greet him. He tells them to take a seat as he settles into his chair behind his ornate desk. Christopher looks at John.

"John, Mom and I have something to discuss with Father James. Why don't you go outside and play with the other kids."

John is disappointed as he likes to hear what his dad discusses, but he never argues with him.

"Sure, Dad. See you outside."

He heads down the hall, wondering what could be so important that they had to have a private meeting with Father James. John's curiosity gets the better of him and he turns back and quietly listens through the open door.

Father James pours a glass of water, offering some to Christopher and Mary.

"It's nice to see you both. What can I do for you?"

Christopher comes right to the point.

"Well, Father, as you probably know, we are facing a financially difficult time right now.."

"Yes, I have heard. But I assure you that with enough prayer, you will receive an answer."

Mary chimes in. "We pray every day, Father, but we need the church's help."

Father James leans back in his chair. "I am not sure what we can do for you."

Christopher leans forward. "Father, we need to borrow some money until we can get back on our feet."

"I see. Christopher, as you know, the church survives on the generous contributions of its members. We really don't have a surplus of money to give out to..."

Christopher interrupts, "Father, we are not asking for a handout. We want to take a loan and are willing to pay interest. We barely have enough money to feed ourselves, let alone make this a merry Christmas for John."

Father James exhales slowly, gathering his thoughts.

"Christopher, Mary, I want to share something with you, but I ask that you keep it in the strictest of confidence."

Outside the door, John has heard enough. He walks away. Halfway down the hall he violently kicks a trashcan.

"Whatever happened to helping your fellow man? I don't trust anybody anymore. I am going to find a way never to be poor again, no matter what I have to do or who I have to crush to get what I want. And I am done with church."

Outside some of the neighborhood kids are playing a game of tag when John slams the door open. They all stop and look at him. The boys gather and start trading rude comments among themselves. Some giggling erupts.

John's anger is more than he can manage. "What's so funny, jerks?"

Jack, the neighborhood bully, replies with a challenge. "Who you calling jerks?"

Charlie, Jack's sidekick and a boy who is scared of his own shadow, jumps in.

"I'll tell you what's funny. Those clothes, that's what."

John looks down at his tattered clothing and pants that barely reach his shoes. Sam, the wise guy of the group, points at John's pants.

"Hey, didn't your mama invite your pants to meet your shoes?"

Adding insult to injury, Charlie spouts, "What's your dad cooking for dinner tonight, your dog? Oh, wait, that's right, you are too poor to own a dog. Maybe your mama can shoot a squirrel and cook that."

The boys crack themselves up, laughing and pointing at John. That is the last straw. John's neck bulges with adrenaline and mounting blood pressure. Losing all control, John yells a commando scream and runs at Charlie, landing a punch squarely in his face. A fight ensues. Both boys get in shots at each other, but Charlie gets the worst of it. John eventually gets Charlie on the ground and repeatedly punches him in the face.

"I... *PUNCH* will... *PUNCH* be... *PUNCH* rich... *PUNCH* and... *PUNCH* powerful... *PUNCH*."

John grabs the boy by his shirt and pulls him close to his face.

"You won't be worth the dirt on this ground. I will buy your family's house and burn it to the ground while you watch."

Jack tries to pull John off Charlie and gets a punch in the eye for his trouble. John turns his attention back to Charlie and raises his fist to continue punching him when John hears his mother's voice screaming at him.

"John! John Daily, stop that this instant."

John looks over his shoulder and sees his parents standing there. He wipes his forehead with his bloodied hands, smearing blood across it. He looks at Charlie, who is crying and very bloody. He leans in nose to nose.

"Don't ever say another word about my family again or I will finish what I started."

He gets off Charlie, stands up, and gives him a last kick to make sure he got the message.

Chapter Three

John is a high school senior graduating at the top of his class. Having been accepted to every school he applied to, his choice leads him to New York City. With his high academic achievements, he has garnished a full scholarship to attend NYU business school.

When the day arrives, there are tears as he boards the train to New York. The train ride gives John time to reflect on the life he is leaving behind, especially his mom and dad. Memories flood his mind, filling him with both love and sorrow, knowing his future is one in which his parents are no longer there on a daily basis. He can always call, but it won't be like having them close. He smiles, thinking about the CARE packages his mother will send from time to time, shipments of cookies that he will secretly hide for his sole enjoyment. The last memory that visits him before he nods off is of the Christmas he received the bike from Santa. He recalls standing in front of the Christmas village where he made his solemn vow to help all the villagers as his parents looked on with pride and love.

The train conductor walks down the aisle announcing they have arrived at their last stop, Penn Station in New York City. Excited about his new life as a college student, he quickly figures out how to get to NYU by subway. Having very little luggage to carry makes it easier.

Arriving at the campus, he is greeted by a resident assistant who promptly shows him his room, gives him a schedule, and explains the house rules.

John thanks him and begins to unpack. He puts away his belongings, makes his bed, and heads to orientation. As he enters the hall, he can't help but notice the other kids are dressed far better than he. John is a bit self-conscious and embarrassed, but he refuses to give up. He sits apart from what appears to be the "in crowd" so as to not draw attention. Waiting for the orientation to begin, his thoughts return to his parents and to all the sacrifices they made over the years to give him the best childhood they could. He has no regrets and loves the farm where he was raised. A smile comes across his face, followed by an overwhelming sense of pride and confidence. At that moment he realizes a boy is sitting next to him. John glances over and sees that he isn't wearing the best clothes either.

"Hi, my name is John. What's yours?"

"Ted. Nice to meet you. What are you here for?"

"Business. You?"

"Entertainment."

John smiles. "Sounds exciting. Are you going to make movies?"

"With any luck I will. What do you want to do with your major?"

"I want to become the richest person in the country."

Ted smiles. "That's quite an aspiration. If you succeed, you want to finance my films?"

They both laugh and in no time become tight friends. Ted starts making short films that John enjoys watching while offering Ted his critique. Ted is appreciative of John's honesty and makes changes in his approach to the script and how he will shoot future projects.

The following semester, they decide to become roommates. Since they both came from poor backgrounds, they challenge each other relentlessly. They know they have to push hard to be on equal ground with the privileged kids who had attended expensive private schools. Neither one of them envies those kids, but they know that if they work hard then the results will be the only thing they will be judged on in the real world. They make sure neither one of them ever gives up, no matter how difficult it becomes.

With their noses to the grindstone for the entire four years and graduation only months away, they both have secured post-collegiate job offers. Ted is approached by a top agency representing writers and directors. He goes on to become a very successful filmmaker.

John is offered a director position in a global import business. It is a match made in heaven. While working late one night, John notices an undetected fault in the company workflow that is creating a bottleneck and draining profits. John takes a gamble and asks to see the CEO. It is a very risky move because his boss had made it very clear that all communications needed to go through him. John's boss is known to steal ideas from the new guys in order to earn accolades from the higher ups. John isn't about to have any of his ideas stolen and not get the credit that is due him. He succeeds in getting a meeting with the CEO.

On the day of the meeting he walks into the office of Mr. Roberts, who, like all CEOs, is busy reviewing papers. He tells John to have a seat. A minute later, and without looking up, Mr. Roberts asks what John wanted to talk with him about, since he wouldn't tell his secretary. John explains in a carefully worded and professional presentation how the profit margin is being drained because of a flaw in the company workflow--one that is going unchecked. As John goes into detail on his finding, Mr. Roberts stops what he is doing and looks up at him. John is straight faced, serious, and very much on point. Two days later, and after a severe admonishment from his boss, John is named the new VP in charge of global strategy. He will be reporting to Mr. Roberts directly.

Over the years, John comes to realize he has a natural flair for finding money that is being drained in every corner of the business. He is offered a partnership, but he turns it down to start his own global company called Daily Investments.

John's announcement to the press is so well received by his current clients that they decide to work with him directly. The work load is more than he can handle, so he begins ramping up and employing the best people he can afford. His diversity in multiple businesses spreads quickly in the global market.

One night while having a quiet cocktail, he sits next to a very attractive woman. She turns to him and introduces herself.

"Hi, my name is Katherine. I see you in here quite a bit. Are you local?"

He extends his hand. "Hi, I'm John. Yes, I live close by. And you?"

"Local as they come."

He is immediately smitten by her looks, although her intellect is more intriguing. They spend several hours that night discussing every topic under the sun. It is a fun time for both since they are on the same page with politics, religion, family values, and recreation. The only difference between them is that Katherine comes from a privileged background whereas John comes from a farm.

During the time it takes to get to know each other, Katherine never makes an issue about money and always makes John feel like an equal. She is not a gold digger looking for someone to fit into a traditional and financial box. She prefers love and honesty, both of which John has in abundance.

Their courtship is old school, which suits them

perfectly. They both want to take it slow, get to know each other, enjoy the courtship, and laugh a lot. John is charming, sincere, gentlemanly, funny, and falling in love. Katherine is intelligent, beautiful, athletic, caring, loyal, and is also falling in love. As time goes on, John begins to accumulate the wealth he always wanted. When he feels financially stable, he decides to ask Katherine to marry him.

The night arrives on which John will pop the question. He creates a romantic evening accented with candles, a bottle of wine, and dinner cooking on the stove. Once the dishes are cleared off the table, John gathers his courage. He takes out a ring box gets down on one knee, opens it, and proposes. Katherine looks at him and says nothing. John's heart almost stops, thinking she is searching for a way to say no without causing him too much pain.

"What took you so long?" she blurts out.

John looks at her smiling at him with tears in her eyes and arms open to receive his hug and kiss to consummate the proposal. They both crack up laughing. It is the natural next step. Everything they do together usually winds up with them laughing and hugging. They are ready for marriage and a family.

"John, you shouldn't have bought a ring. How did you know I would say yes?"

John smiles mischievously. It is now his turn to tease her.

"Don't worry, it comes with a thirty-day money-back guarantee."

She punches him in the arm.

"Very funny, John."

"You know, Katherine, my only regret is that my mom never got to meet you. But at least you know my dad."

"And he is a wonderful man. I know I would have loved your mom, too."

She wraps her arms around him and hugs him tightly, assuring him their life together will be beautiful.

Chapter Four

On an overcast day with a light drizzle, a limousine, a few local cars, and trucks line an off-road area. It is the local cemetery, and its battered tombstones show years of wear from the harsh weather. Black umbrellas surround an open grave. Rolling thunder echoes through the nearby hills as Father James speaks words of comfort.

"He was a good shepherd of the Lord. Christopher lived a good life and always had love in his heart for his fellow man and especially for his family."

Thirty-seven-year-old John stands next to Katherine, who is dressed elegantly. Standing next to

Katherine are their two children—seven-year-old Angela, wearing a darling dress and holding a small purse, and nine-year-old Beau, dressed in a suit and a bow tie. Both stay close to Katherine as Father James finishes his sermon. John stands there silent and sad.

"His love for his wife and his son John will live on. As we lay Christopher to rest, let's remember all the good he brought to the world. Amen."

All reply, "Amen,"

Two of the local women who knew the family are whispering to each other.

"Can't imagine the pain he is going through," Mrs. Mulroy whispers to Mrs. Laughton.

Mrs. Laughton raises an eyebrow. "I know, especially since his mom died before he became so rich."

"Yes, his money could have gotten her the medical care she needed to save her life," she says with a flit of her hand.

Mrs. Laughton narrows her eyes. "I hear he is a ruthless businessman."

Father James joins John and his family.

"My condolences for your loss. He was a great man. How is New York treating you, John?"

John ignores the question. "I should have been here for Dad."

Father James pauses. "You shouldn't feel guilty about this. You couldn't have known he would have a heart attack in his sleep. No one could. At least it was painless. May his soul rest in peace."

An uncomfortable silence stretches between them. John stares into the open grave where his dad's coffin lays. Beneath the coffin rests his mother's casket. The sight creates a double rip in John's saddened heart. He feels like an orphan. John's dad once told him that while your parent are alive, they form a protective barrier between children and the grim reaper. Now it is John's time to step into that spot, and he does so uncomfortably.

Father James wants to comfort John in his time of grief but knows how he feels toward the church. Father James makes an attempt to reach him.

"If there is anything I can do, please let me know or stop by the church. You are always welcome."

John's face grows taut but he says nothing. His anger toward the church and religion is legendary in the community, and Father James is no stranger to these feelings. Katherine senses the tension between them and steps in to defuse the situation.

"Thank you, Father James. We appreciate all you have done."

Father James gives an understanding nod and

walks away, leaving John and his family by the grave. John watches him depart.

"Honey, would you mind taking the kids to the car? I want to be alone for a minute."

The pain she senses in John and the love for his dad brings tears to her eyes, and she touches his arm gingerly.

"Of course, sweetheart."

She kisses him and leads the kids to the car. John looks down once again. A gentle rain starts to fall. John struggles to get the words out of his mouth.

"Dad, I'm sorry I didn't have a chance to say goodbye. I miss mom so much... and now you. I will always love you and mom more than anything else in the whole wide world."

John falls to his knees and grabs a handful of earth. He pours it out of his hands onto the coffin.

Mr. Miller, the pawn shop owner, approaches John as he stands and brushes the damp dirt from his knees. He wears a raincoat and hat, with no umbrella.

"Excuse me, John."

John turns around. "I'm sorry, do we know each other?"

Mr. Miller shakes his head. "No, but I knew your father very well. He was a good man and made a lot of people feel good about the simple life we live here."

John replies politely, "I appreciate that." He starts to walk away.

Mr. Miller calls after him, "Can I have a minute? I have something for you."

John is not sure what to make of this man. He becomes suspicious because everyone knows John is a rich man and people are always asking him for donations or for money to fund their projects.

Mr. Miller looks into John's eyes and picks up on it. "John, you misunderstand my intentions. I don't want anything from you. I want to give you something."

Mr. Miller reaches into his overcoat pocket. John takes a tiny step backwards, unsure whether to run or to play this out.

Mr. Miller pulls out something that is wrapped in a handkerchief and hands it to John.

"What is this?" John asks as he begins to unwrap it.

Mr. Miller watches. "I have held onto this for 30 years in hopes of one day giving it back to your dad."

It is his dad's old watch.

"I don't understand. How did you...why do you have it?"

Mr. Miller recounts the event. "Many years ago when you were a small boy your dad came into my pawn shop. He wanted to give you a bicycle for Christmas but times were very tough. Hell, they never improved, which is why I still have that watch. He was never in a financial position to come back and retrieve it, but at the same time I could never bring myself to sell it either."

"I'm confused. I paid off the farm and sent him money every month."

Mr. Miller smiles. "I know. But your father was a very proud man and never wanted anyone to know what he had done. We just kept this between us. He told people that the watch was lost. For him it was best if he just left things alone."

As tears form in his eyes, he says, "What do I owe you on behalf of my dad?"

"Nothing. Consider it a gift. Maybe someday it will do you or someone else some good."

Mr. Miller extends his hand, and John shakes it. He watches from his father's graveside as Mr. Miller walks away. Thunder and lightning pierce the silence of the setting.

Chapter Five

Across the Hudson River, on a crisp winter day, the New York City skyline stands vibrant and proud. Steam rises from hot vents in the street as the crowds hustle past one another on their way to work. Horse-drawn carriages loaded with tourists stroll through Central Park. The museums are open for the art lovers, people compete for the next available cab, while others rush to get on the subway heading toward their destination. The noise of the city swells into a cacophony of music.

A limousine pulls up to one of the tallest and most famous buildings in New York City. The building sign reads "Daily Global Investments." Inside the grand lobby are some of the most beautiful models the world has to offer. The place bristles with energy as assistants hasten to and fro. Clothing is being sorted through in preparation for the next shoot. Some models are dressed in bathing suits while others are getting fitted in furs. Photographers snap orders at their assistants, who respond with lightning speed. Amid the chaos are well dressed business people in custom-made clothing, each toting a briefcase and ready to meet the challenges of another business day.

A limo driver opens the door and John steps out and heads into the building. As he walks through the lobby he is greeted by all. He goes directly to his private elevator that will take him to the penthouse floor. When the doors open he is greeted by his assistant, Laura. She is in her twenties, sharp as a tack, attractive, and dressed in corporate attire. She is one of the youngest high-level assistants in the city. John likes her because he sees a lot of himself in her, and she knows that mistakes made while working for John make for a quick trip to the unemployment line. There are no second chances, no excuses, only impeccable performance is acceptable. Laura hands John his morning cup of coffee--a double latté, two sugars, one spoon of whipped cream, and very hot.

She briefs him on the day's agenda during the walk to his office. John enters his office and Laura goes to her desk.

John is looking out his window at the view of New York, which seems to calm him, when Laura buzzes over the intercom that he has an important call on line one. Still staring out the window, he picks up the phone and listens. His face turns red and his hand squeezes the receiver. He does not take bad news well.

"How many times do I have to tell you? I don't give a rat's ass what the issue is, just get it taken care of or you can find another job!"

The caller persists but John cuts him off. "I don't care about that either. I have seventy floors with thirty different businesses. I don't have time for your problems!" He slams the phone down.

Laura knocks cautiously on the door to his office.

John turns and sees her. "What now?

"It's your wife on line two."

John doesn't want to deal with anything at the moment. "I'll have to call her back."

Laura speaks softly. "She said it was important."

John takes a step forward. "I'll decide what's important. Now get out of my office. I have a call to make."

Laura backs out of his office quickly. She goes to

her desk, picks up the phone, and pushes the line on hold.

"Hi, Katherine. I'm sorry but he is tied up on an important call."

Katherine is at home, busy with the day's activities of running the estate.

"Sounds like he is in one of his pleasant moods."

Laura is appreciative of Katherine's understanding of John's mood swings.

"I'm afraid so. He has every top model in New York in here today for a shoot."

All Katherine can do is shake her head and take a deep, relaxing breath.

"Man's going to give himself a heart attack. You would have thought he learned his lesson from his dad."

Laura nods. "I agree. He takes every one of his businesses very seriously and is totally hands on. Even if the business is only a 20-million dollar account." Laura sees John approaching her desk.
"Sorry, Katherine... gotta go," she whispers and hangs up the phone just as John reaches her desk.

"Get me the file on the Alexander account and put it in the conference room. I have to see what that diva photographer is up to. Got a call from one of the model's agents about abuse."

Walking away, Laura can hear him say under his breath, "I like that guy."

John walks into the shoot and stands off to one side, watching. An attractive model in her early twenties sits in a chair and strikes an uncomfortable-looking pose. She is dressed to the nines in high-end clothing and has a jaw-dropping hairstyle created by one of the best in the entertainment industry. The crew is working on her makeup, rearranging her dress, and touching up her hair. All the while the photographer is growing impatient.

"Pull the strap down more off her right shoulder."

The wardrobe person jumps into action, adjusting the straps. The photographer is still unhappy with the results.

"More, you twit. I want to see more of her shoulder."

The wardrobe person makes further adjustments. The model is clearly upset at the constant yelling and the temper of the photographer. Although she is a professional, he has brought her to the edge of her nerves.

Looking through the lens of the camera, the photographer sees something else he doesn't like.

"Didn't I tell you to yank the dress up over her thigh? I need to see that long leg we are paying over-scale for."

Once again the wardrobe person runs into frame and makes more adjustments.

"How's that?"

"Fine, now straighten out her dress. It's a mess."

The wardrobe person does as asked.

"How's that?"

The photographer addresses the model. "Turn more towards the light."

The model is awkward and loses her balance as she turns, causing the photographer to lose what little patience he has.

"You've got to be joking. Where did you learn to model, at K-Mart?" He takes an intimidating step toward her. "If I wanted to work with an uncoordinated amateur I could have hired one of my sister's idiotic friends."

The model has reached her saturation point and breaks down crying. With an utter lack of sympathy the photographer steps closer to her.

"Oh, great. Here we go. Your ruining your makeup, you frickin' moron."

The model glances around the room and sees John in the shadows of the stage. Totally embarrassed, she runs off the set and out the door. John goes over to the photographer.

"I see you handled that really well."

The photographer hears John's voice and turns around.

"Hey, Mr. Daily. Models today are so sensitive."

John smiles. "Yeah, well, we got another call from her agent claiming abuse. Frankly I didn't see anything, if you get my meaning."

"Okay. So you want me to coddle her?"

"No. Do what you have to do to get the best shots. Maybe get a different model."

John walks off the set and heads toward the elevator. His cell phone rings, and he sees it is Katherine. He pushes ignore and puts the phone back in his coat pocket. He heads to the conference room for a briefing from his key executives.

The tension in the room is so thick it is hard to catch a decent breath of air. The conference room is state of the art, with a large handmade granite table perfectly honed at the edges to give it a design quality of the finest craftsmanship. The room has a large conference screen, a voice-activated conference call system, shades that are electronically operated, and all of it accented with chairs upholstered with the finest Italian leather.

John takes his seat at the head of the table. The room is filled with anxious-looking executives. They know John is a force to be reckoned with and there are no excuses for underperforming. Today is the day that financial reports are due for many of his businesses. This is the first of many meetings scheduled for the day. John doesn't waste a minute, nor does he engage in small talk as he takes a seat.

"Jeff, what's your report on our market share?"

Jeff is in his mid-twenties and is a statistics wizard. He was hand-plucked from one of the best business schools in the country before he graduated. He has a computer-like mind, with details flowing like lava. He opens his folder with what he thinks will be received as excellent work. He is ready to be praised.

"We are currently at a 77 percent market share for the first two quarters. Our third quarter, which ends next week, promises to go to 79 percent."

John pauses for a second and looks around the room. "Good news. I want to see 80 percent by year-end."

Murmurs fill the room. If that isn't good enough to get John's praise, the rest of the executives know firsthand their fates are on thin ice.

John furls his eyebrows at the sound of murmurs. "Anyone have a problem with that?"

No one dares to answer.

"Good." He points toward the door. "As you know

that's the way to the unemployment line. Ralph, how are our European business numbers so far this year?"

Ralph is a very proud man in his late thirties and speaks with a German accent. He shifts in his chair uncomfortably, knowing what is about to happen.

"As we all know--"

John interrupts him immediately. "Don't drag the rest of us into your report."

Ralph continues. "MSNBC has been reporting a slowdown in the European sectors due to banking issues throughout Europe, and as a result..."

John begins to lose his patience. "Cut the dance lessons, Ralph. What are the numbers?"

Ralph points to his open file. "It's not that simple, Mr. Daily. We have to take into account what the market can bear. Shipping exports is a very tricky business and..."

John's face becomes very stern and emotionless.

"I'm not going to ask you again."

Ralph is cornered and has to address the inevitable.

"We have lost 3.5 percent year to date."

John lowers his head. The others in the room try not looking at Ralph, who appears desperate for any show of support.

John lifts his head and glares at Ralph.

"You are on a plane tonight to our European office. I want this changed before you return or don't come back. Am I clear?"

An intimidated Ralph ekes out a, "Yes, sir."

John looks over the room and stops his scan on Yamachi; late thirties, wearing large black-rimmed glasses. John's focus is penetrating.

"What's going on in our Asian market?"

Yamachi's forehead is covered with beads of sweat. He pulls out his handkerchief and wipes it dry.

"Ah, Mr. Daily-san, I aflaid I have not so good news."

John doesn't hesitate. "Plane. Tonight."

Respectfully Yamachi bows his head. "Hai, Mr. Daily-san.

At the conclusion of the meeting John does not say a word. He stands up and leaves the room. He walks down the hall and stops at Laura's desk.

"Laura, notify the restaurant I am on my way for lunch."

Laura picks up the phone. "Yes, Mr. Daily."

John walks through the perpetually busy lobby, with everyone greeting him as if he were royalty. He leaves the building. His limo standing by.

John's driver greets him.

"Good afternoon, Mr. Daily. All set to take you to

lunch, sir."

Today John has a different idea. "I'm going to walk. I'll see you later."

The limo driver is a bit perplexed but never engages in small talk with John.

"Yes, sir."

As John heads down the street his cell phone rings. The caller ID shows it is Katherine again. He pushes ignore and continues to walk. The phone rings again. It is from his daughter, Angela. He pushes ignore and continues down the street. It rings again. It's his son, Beau. He hits ignore. The caller ID shows PAMA Investments. He answers the call.

"Marty. How is our new IPO coming along?" John continues toward the restaurant.

Although he is well bundled against the cold, each breath is visible as the warm moisture coming from his nostrils hits the frigid air. He continues strolling down the street, engrossed in a conversation with his broker about his new IPO promising huge profits for one of his companies. John is obsessed with making deals turn into large sums of money. He welcomes competition and beats them all hands down. Nothing makes him happier. He has reached his childhood goal as the wealthiest man in America.

As John approaches one of New York's finest

restaurants, the doorman promptly opens the door and wears a warm, welcoming smile. He greets John as the restaurant's most valuable client. As he enters, the maître d' scurries over to John to receive his coat, scarf, and gloves. He escorts him to his standing reserved table in the corner where he has maximum privacy. John says goodbye to Marty, ends the call, and takes his seat as the maître d' pushes in his chair. He is immediately handed a menu. Most of the patrons in the restaurant recognize him from the news and the multitude of magazine covers he has been featured on in connection to articles touting his enormous success.

A patron turns to her companion. "You know who that is?"

With a smug smile her companion says, "Of course I do, sweetie. He is the most powerful man in America. Although I hear he isn't the most pleasant person to do business with."

"Yes, I have heard the same thing about him. Ruthless, indeed."

Other patrons glance over at John while he reads the menu. His cell phone rings. It is Beau again. Once again he hits ignore and goes back to the menu. As he does, a very large woman approaches his table.

"Mr. Daily?"

John looks up from his menu. He thinks this is not going to be enjoyable.

"Yes."

She points to her table, where there are several other well dressed women. All of them smile and wave at him.

"Our group is here from the Midwest for a convention, and we would love to get a picture with you and an autograph."

Just as John suspected. Another annoying person wanting his autograph, as if he were a rock star or a famous celebrity. He is a businessman who demands his privacy. John glances over at the maître d' with wide eyes. The maître d' rushes over to the woman.

"Excuse me, ma'am, but Mr. Daily would prefer to be left alone while he dines."

She looks at John. He gives her a half-smile, reinforcing the maître d's words.

The woman's smile turns to a frown. She looks the maître d' up and down.

"Well, all we wanted was a picture and autograph. Is that too much to ask?"

John has had enough of this exchange.

"Yes, it is."

The woman walks back to her table in a huff and explains to her friends what just happened. They all glare over at John, who is now speaking with the maître d'.

"My apology, Mr. Daily."

"Do I need to find another restaurant who will take better care of me?"

"No, sir. I assure you this will not happen again."

"Fine. Martini with two olives."

The maître d' is relieved. "Right away."

John never misses an opportunity to save money.

"On the house for the inconvenience."

"Of course. My pleasure."

After lunch John heads down a quiet street on his way back to his office. He is lost in thought, ruminating about his new IPO and the amount of money it will raise at the opening bell on Wall Street. He starts to strategize about opening a new division in one of his companies that has proven to be a major moneymaker in the manufacturing sector. He rounds the corner heading toward his office when a bum staggers out from a doorway and approaches him. The man has his hand in his pocket, suggesting that he is holding a gun.

"If you want to live you will give me your money."

John is amused and looks him over. The bum stands there unsteadily. John grins and shakes his head.

"You're holding me up? You want my money?"

"What's the matter, you don't speak English?" the bum says, swaying a bit.

John decides to teach this guy a lesson. He looks past the bum, tilting his head to one side. As his curiosity wins out, the bum turns around to see what John is looking at. The bum sees nothing. He turns back around just in time for John's fist to connect squarely with his face. The bum goes down with a fat, bloodied lip. John kicks him several times. His anger gets the better of him, and he imagines himself kicking the church boy who said bad things about his family.

"Try to steal my money, you piece of dirt. Don't you ever say anything bad about my family again."

The bum is confused and covers his face. "I never said anything about your family. I only wanted money for food."

John gathers his thoughts, but is still angry about his run-in with the low-life who tried to rob him.

"Right! And that retched smell of liquor is your current cologne?"

John kicks the bum again before walking away. Bloodied and beat, the bum screams after John.

"I hope someday you know what it's like to have nothing."

John turns back and takes a step toward the

bum, who covers up, fearful of more abuse.

"I came from nothing. No one gave me squat. Try working for a living like the rest of us." John turns and walks away.

In a meek voice the bum says, "I was a VP and lost everything and now I live on the street."

Without looking back John says, "Let me get my violin, loser."

The Daily family are seated at the dinner table finishing their meal when the front door opens and John comes in.

Beau looks at Angela with an ear to ear smile. "Daddy's home."

Both kids run over to him and give him a hug. Katherine smiles at the sight of their affection for their father. She knows he loves them although he never seems to find quality time to spend with them doing things a father should be doing. John returns the hug and kisses Beau and Angela.

"You kids have a good day at school?"

Angela puts her hands on her hips in her sassy way.

"Yes, except for you not answering my call."

Katherine chimes in from across the room.

"Or mine."

Beau piles on. "Same here, Dad."

John walks the kids back to the table. He takes his seat and smiles at Katherine, who continues to press the point.

"We were starting to worry about you, John."

John knows he is busted but is always able to counter their moves and skillfully manages to change the subject.

"Rough day at the office. I ran from one floor to another all day. Prima donna models, agents calling, corporate quarterly reports, complex deals pending-- you know, the usual pressures. What's for dinner?"

Katherine has seen this act many times before but decides to let it go.

"We decided to make your favorite dish."

Trying to be cute, John responds with, "And what restaurant would that be?"

Katherine squints her eyes at him. Angela's head spins toward John.

"Daddy, don't you know your favorite dish?"

Beau chimes in to defend his dad.

"He's just kidding."

Katherine's smile is sarcastic. "Meatloaf. I know it's not exactly like your mom used to make, but we did the best we could."

John attempts more humor.

"So, does that mean we ARE going out to dinner?"

Both kids jump in.

"DADDY!"

Katherine decides the game's afoot and that this is a good time for the kids to ask John what they have been waiting to ask him.

"Very funny, John. Kids, didn't you want to ask your father a question?"

John looks at Katherine, not sure what to expect.

Angela speaks first. "Daddy, can we please build the Christmas village this year?"

John looks sternly at Katherine. She smiles back at him, knowing he will not engage in a heated debate in front of the kids. He stares at her with eyes that say, *We need to discuss what just happened and I'm not happy about being ambushed.*

"Well, first of all, Christmas is a few months away, and time is kind of tight around the holidays with work."

With a disappointed look on his face Beau eyes his sister.

"Told you he would have another excuse."

Katherine sees their disappointed little faces and jumps in to help try to convince him.

"John, really. You have been promising the kids for several years to put it up. They love that village."

"Can we talk about this later?"

Angela softly says to Beau, "I know what that means. The parents go off to talk and then no village."

John tries to explain to Beau and Angela.

"Kids, listen. I work really long hours, and to build that village brings with it certain..."

"*Memories* is the word you are looking for. Memories that you should be passing on to our children like your parents did with you..and besides--"

John is aggravated and cuts her off sternly. "Katherine... Can we discuss this later?"

It becomes very quiet. The kids look at Katherine.

"Very well, John. Why don't you serve yourself some dinner. I'll get the kids their desert."

After dinner, Katherine cleans up the kitchen while the kids get ready for bed. They know the routine and go directly to their rooms, change into their pajamas, and brush their teeth. John sits in his chair in the family den and goes through emails. He knows exactly how much time is left before he and Katherine tuck the kids in, and he wants to make every second count. He loves the deal-making process and is absorbed in it every waking minute. He lives for the adrenaline rush when the deal closes and the bank account rises.

John continues to work on his cell phone until he hears Katherine calling him from upstairs. He finishes his last email then puts his phone in his pocket for retrieval later that night. He is obsessed with his businesses, and nothing will stop him or get between him and his ambition. He will never be poor again. The caveat is that although John is rich in money he is poor in emotions, but he doesn't see this, just like he doesn't see the toll it has taken on his family over the years.

Katherine tries at every turn to bring the man she fell in love with back to his senses and his loving family. Again Katherine calls to him. He gets up and makes the trek upstairs.

Angela's bedroom is decorated in a way every girl dreams. It looks like the castle of a princess. The pink room with a lace canopy over the bed is a fairytale come to life. There is a dressing room with a walk-in closet the size of most bedrooms. In one corner of the room sits a three-panel mirrored table for her to sit at and fix her hair. Someday it will also provide the perfect light for applying her make-up and trying on jewelry.

Angela is on her knees finishing her prayers with John and Katherine looking on.

"And God bless mommy and daddy and all the people in the world." She climbs into bed.

Katherine tucks her in, kisses her goodnight, and

makes way for John. He reaches down and kisses her on the forehead.

"Goodnight, princess."

She looks up with soft eyes that would melt the hardest of hearts. John can't help but smile at his daughter. He strokes her hair, as does Katherine, and leaves her room.

Beau's bedroom is fully equipped with all the latest gadgets, including a large flat-screen TV, every game console on the market, a wall filled with video games, another wall filled with books--because, unlike many of the other boys, Beau has an insatiable appetite for knowledge just like John had when he was a small boy--shelves of sports trophies, space models hanging from the ceiling, signed baseballs, basketballs, and footballs from the most famous players in history, and a dressing room closet the same size as Angela's. Katherine and John stand close by as Beau finishes his nightly prayer.

"Amen."

Beau springs up off his knees then drops right back down.

"Oh, also, would you please tell Daddy to build the village this year? Amen... again."

Katherine sees John's face tighten at the sound of Beau's prayer addendum. Tonight Katherine will make yet another attempt at getting John to build the Christmas village in order to pass on what has been handed down to him from generation to generation. Over the years, the family has added to the Dickens village collection. It has grown so large that it sits on a platform constructed from three-quarter-inch plywood on top of sawhorses. It has to be strong enough to support two people standing on top to place trees, houses, hand carved mountains made out of Styrofoam, lights, and small figurines throughout the entire layout.

Katherine knows there is tension every time the topic of the village is brought up, but she refuses to give up on the family tradition, which the kids love and will ultimately become part of their childhood memories.

John goes over to Beau. "Keep up the great work at school and in sports. You make me very proud."

He bends down to kiss Beau, who wraps his arms around his dad.

"I want to be just like you when I grow up."

He smiles at his son as Katherine leans in to kiss Beau goodnight. Katherine and John leave Beau's room, closing the door behind them. Outside of Beau's room John confronts Katherine.

"I wish you would stop encouraging them about

that stupid village."

She puts her finger to her lips and points toward their bedroom. John nods his head.

Their bedroom is spacious and elegantly decorated. Plush curtains made from the world's most luxurious material are accented with rare antiquities and priceless works of art hanging on the walls. Their king-size headboard was hand-carved by the world famous craftsman Louis Manqué, who was flown in from Paris to make the frame specifically for them. The well cushioned carpet is silk and laced with gold thread. No television can be seen, but with the touch of a button a section of the wall opens revealing a sixty-inch screen complete with 5.1 Dolby surround sound. Katherine enters the room followed by John, who closes the door so that the kids will not overhear their discussion.

Without hesitation and very upset, Katherine blurts out to John, "That stupid village was handed down to you by your father and from his father. And you yourself continued the tradition for so long - then you stopped. I never understood why. You know how much it means to them. Why not build it with them this Christmas? You know, spend quality time with your kids."

John is frustrated. Not so much by the village as

by his inner demons, haunting him about his family's struggle during his childhood, when he vowed to never be poor again.

"Enough about the village. I don't have the time. After all, someone has to make the money around here."

Katherine is incensed.

"So spending time with your family is a waste of time? How much is enough, John? You are the wealthiest man in America."

John has heard this dozens of times.

"Here we go again."

Katherine doesn't back down.

"Yes, damn it, here we go again. I don't know what has happened to you, but you have turned into this obsessive man... and for what? So you can take over the entire world? I just don't get it."

John is annoyed that he has to have this conversation again.

"No one left anything for me or my mom or dad. Where were all the well-wishers then?"

"So this is about payback?" she replies.

"It's not like that, Katherine. When mom and dad were alive we had nothing. Hardly any food. Mom wore clothes that she got from the secondhand store. We were poorer than poor."

"Well, you're not anymore. You need to spend more time with the kids."

John softens at the thought.

"Yeah, I know, but the businesses..."

"STOP! Never put your business before your family. Nothing good can come of it."

Cornered, he goes on the attack.

"Easy for you to say. You came from an affluent family."

That is a knife in her heart because she has never used her family's money against John since they first met and fell in love. She stares at him with disdain. She turns, walks into the bathroom, slams the door, and locks it behind her.

John can only stand there knowing he crossed the line.

"Just perfect."

A light snow falls as a limo pulls up to the front of the Daily Global Investment building. A priest stands waiting patiently at the door. The driver opens the door of the limo and John steps out. He sees the priest approaching.

"Oh boy, here comes the church in all their needy glory."

Father Theo knows the Daily family because they are part of his congregation--all except John. Father

Theo is a kind man. He is bundled against the cold and falling snow but refuses to give up on John.

"Good morning, Mr. Daily. May I have a word with you?"

John has no kind words to say to any priest so it isn't personal. Whenever he sees a priest or a church he is drawn back to his childhood, when the church refused to help his family in their moment of deepest need.

"Father, listen, we go through this every so often and I always say the same thing."

"I know, son, but the church is beginning to prepare for Christmas, and the orphans could use some Christmas cheer. Some hope."

John tries to wrap up the conversation as quickly as possible.

"Maybe you should give it a rest.

"You have been blessed with so much, and you are now in a position to help so many."

John stiffens. "Let me ask you something, Father Theo. Where was God when I was growing up? Where was he when my folks needed help? For that matter, where was the church? I'll tell you where. The church, knowing full well we barely had any food on the table, had the audacity to ask for a donation every Sunday. Did the church ever take any of that money and offer relief to my folks? NO. Not one dime did they offer. Not one meal. No clothes and certainly no money to help pay the mortgage. They offered prayer instead. My mother might still be alive if they had reached out. Now you can pray all you want and find another sucker for your cause. And you can tell God I said so."

John walks away and enters the building. The limo driver approaches Father Theo and hands him a twenty-dollar bill.

"Here, Father. It's all I can afford. I hope it helps."

"Bless you, son. He is a tortured soul, and I am afraid he is in for a very hard lesson someday."

John walks through the spacious lobby headed toward his private elevator. He passes a large-screen monitor and hears the announcer.

"With almost two months left before Christmas, department stores are reporting shoppers getting an early start on their gift-buying. This year retailers are planning..."

John is at a boiling point as he walks over to the guard.

"Change that channel and NEVER allow anything on that TV that mentions Christmas. Understood!"

The guard is visibly shaken knowing that any discussion would end in termination of his employment.

"Yes, sir." He changes the channel to the weather station.

John gets in his private elevator. On the way up, he lets out a tortured scream. He loosens his tie and unbuttons his collar. Knowing he is losing it, he stops the elevator long enough to regain his composer, button his shirt, and straighten out his tie. After a short time, John re-starts the elevator and continues to the penthouse floor.

Stepping off the elevator, John walks directly to Laura's desk.

"Did you pick up my watch yet?"

Laura has a keen sense and has learned to anticipate his demands. She hands him the watch.

"Here you go, Mr. Daily."

He takes the envelope and walks into his office. Laura mumbles to herself softly, making sure he can't hear her.

"You're welcome."

John sits down at his desk. He picks up a picture of his mom and dad, takes a deep breath, and sets the picture back down. He takes the watch out of the envelope and smiles. It is a bittersweet moment. He now knows the truth about his childhood bicycle. It reinforces the endless love he has for his parents. They gave up so much to make his life as good as possible.

They never complained to John about anything and always encouraged him to do his best in life. Despite the fact they were poorer than dirt, his family always surrounded him with love.

He takes off his Rolex and puts it in his desk drawer. He puts his father's watch on his wrist and watches the second hand tick away. A smile creeps across his face. Laura comes into his office, pauses when she sees him smiling, then gently knocks. His smile immediately disappears.

Holding her tablet, she announces, "Your 10:00 AM appointment is in the conference room."

John doesn't look up at her. "Call the senior executives and make sure they are ready for this presentation."

Laura takes pride in being one step ahead of John.

"Already done. They are in the conference room waiting for you."

John walks past her.

"About time something went right today."

She watches him walk down the hall while shaking her head. She cannot imagine what it would be like to have everything in the world and still be lonely inside.

Chapter Six

Tradition is what binds families and makes memories. Fall ushers in the holidays steeped in multicultural traditions, but none is as celebrated as Thanksgiving. It is a time for all families to join together and express their gratefulness for who they are and what they have.

The chill in the air is the perfect backdrop to cozy up around glowing embers. Turkeys are stuffed with a variety of delicacies and appear like pictures out of recipe books. Candied yams are prepared the day before, and roasted chestnuts are marinated in Grand Marnier for twenty-four hours before being added to the stuffing. Some family members spend hours chopping fresh herbs to combine with either sausage or ground beef as part of the "secret" stuffing recipe passed down from generation to generation. A Bloody Mary with celery, an olive, and a petite onion skewered on a toothpick signal the start of the holiday season and the onset of time spent in front of the fireplace. Playing softly in the background are classic Christmas songs, familiar lyrics filling the air; "Chestnuts roasting on an open fire..." The television highlights the Macy's Day Parade, as a prelude to the traditional Thanksgiving Day football game. During halftime, those who are brave enough gather in the backyard, choose teams for touch football, and scrimmage, which inevitably leads to someone getting grass stains on their nice pants. Such are the spoils of football on Thanksgiving Day.

Every year John and Katherine have Katherine's sister, Sarah, and her family over to share this delicious feast. Sarah is thirty five and dressed for the occasion--simple but elegant. Her husband, Tom, is forty and sports a tie and jacket. His attire reveals a successful businessman, although nowhere near the level that John has achieved. Tom and Sarah have two children. Their seven-year-old daughter, Myra, has golden ringlets and rosy cheeks. She is appropriately outfitted in a silk dress and scarf. Their son, Caleb, is eight, and like his dad he is dressed in a tie and sports jacket. The two families are gathered around the table enjoying their time together, all except for John, who pays no attention as dessert is served.

Sarah sees her sister staring at John and tries to lighten the mood.

"Well, I see you haven't lost your cooking skills. Excellent meal."

Tom joins in as well. "And the wine was fantastic."

The cousins are quietly eating their apple pie and ice cream. They know that once they have finished with dessert they will be excused from the table to go and play. They are oblivious to the mounting tension at the table.

Katherine tries to get John's attention. "John made the stuffing."

He doesn't pick up on Katherine's subtle hint and continues checking his emails under the table.

"John, the stuffing was excellent. Any secret ingredients?" Sarah says.

No response. Sarah looks at Katherine, aware her failed attempt was fully transparent. John continues processing emails, his eyes cast downward, unaware of what is about to come.

"John... John!" Katherine has reached the end of

her patience.

"Sorry, what did you say?" He looks up, knowing he has been busted and instinctively tries to deflect.

"Must you do that at the table? After all, it is Thanksgiving."

"I'm in the middle of an acquisition in Israel and they don't..."

She is perturbed by his weak excuse and poor manners.

"John, I don't really care about any business during dinner."

Everyone looks toward John, but no one makes eye contact with him. John looks at Katherine, then at his kids, and decides not to make an issue out of it. He puts his phone in his jacket pocket and smiles at everyone as if nothing is wrong.

"I think I will go outside for some fresh air." He starts to get up.

"Tom, why don't you join John. Katherine and I will clean up. Kids, you may be excused to go upstairs and play," Sarah suggests.

John looks at Sarah, wanting to say something, but he hesitates. He glances at Katherine, who is not amused, and finally smiles weakly at Tom. The kids start to scramble out of their chairs.

"Caleb, Myra, don't you have something to say?"

Caleb is the first to respond.

"Thanks for a great dinner, Aunt Katherine and Uncle John."

Myra follows her brother's lead.

"Yes, thank you. It was very good. Especially the pie and ice cream."

"You both are very welcome. Can I get a hug and a kiss?" Katherine cannot hide the fact she adores her sister's kids.

They both go over and give her a hug and a kiss. They look toward John and decide not to approach him.

"Excuse me, kids. Are you forgetting someone?" says Sarah.

They look at John, again They go over to him and offer an obligatory hug and kiss.

"Thank you, Uncle John." Caleb hugs and kisses him then runs off with Beau.

Myra looks at John with her soft features and ringlets. She hesitates for a minute.

"Why are you so unhappy, Uncle John? You know Santa knows who is mean to people."

Sarah almost chokes on her dessert.

"MYRA! Apologize to your uncle right this minute."

John looks at Katherine and then at Myra.

"I'm sorry. Thank you for dinner, Uncle John."

She kisses him and runs off, following Angela.

"John, I am so sorry. I have no idea where..."

Before she can finish her sentence, "I'm going outside for some air." He leaves.

"I am really sorry, Katherine. I have no idea why she would say something like that."

Tom can sense it is time the two women engage in a little girl talk.

"I think I will join John for some... some... something." He leaves, giving them their privacy.

Katherine gets up and starts to clean the table. She is visibly shaken.

"You have a very perceptive child. She reminds me of you growing up."

"You mean she says what's on her mind?"

"Exactly."

They both giggle.

"Sis, I've been meaning to ask, where is your staff today?"

Katherine looks in the direction that John went to make sure she isn't overheard.

"Oh, boy. I gave them the day off to be with their families and John flipped. *'Who's going to cook the stupid chicken?'* I had to remind him it was a turkey. Honestly, chicken - turkey, to him it's all the same unless it is cooked by his five-star chef. I wanted this to be a family event, and I am afraid he doesn't know what that means. Either that or he has forgotten what a family is about. I know he loves us all, but..." She starts to cry. Sarah goes to her.

"Come on, sis. Let's go into the kitchen and chat so the kids don't accidently hear us."

Katherine nods, and Sarah takes her hand and leads her into the kitchen.

Katherine starts to make some coffee.

"Hey, forget the coffee. What have you got that has a little kick to it?"

Katherine puts the coffee away. She goes over to the cabinet, opens the door, and pulls out an extremely expensive bottle of single-malt scotch.

Sarah approves. "Now that's the Katherine I know. Which glasses?"

"The tumblers, behind you in the cupboard."

Sarah opens the cupboard and pulls out two tumblers. Katherine pours a double. Sarah looks at her.

"That bad?"

Katherine looks at Sarah with a dazed look in her eyes.

"Makes it a triple."

"Oh, boy. Sit down and take it from the top."

Katherine and Sarah sit and chat in the kitchen,

unaware that John is once again on his cell phone texting. Tom joins him.

"Hope I am not interrupting anything."

John doesn't look up. "Give me a minute to finish this. Have a seat."

Tom takes a seat and occupies his time by looking around the porch. He notices how the railing that separates the porch from the yard is impeccably painted. The wooden floor is finished with a perfectly even sheen. The cushions on the oversized chairs are made from the finest Damask material. Tom thinks about what it must feel like to have so much wealth. He looks at John and can't imagine why he is so disconnected from his family. Tom feels sympathy for John and at the same time envies him. He has often spoken to Sarah about John's situation, and it usually ends with Sarah comforting Tom with respect to his own success. She is very practical and enjoys the comfortable lifestyle Tom has provided. She also understands the delicate male ego when it comes to wanting to provide the very best for the family.

Lost in thought, John speaks to Tom, who has to change his focus.

"This deal in Israel is huge. Worth a ton of dough for my holding companies."

Tom shakes his head to clear his thoughts.

"Exactly how many companies do you own?"

"More than you might imagine."

Upstairs the cousins are playing with each other in their separate bedrooms. A soccer ball slams against the wall, ricocheting back to Beau and Caleb. Caleb assumes his best stance as Beau ducks the oncoming ball.

"That was great."

"Thanks, but I will never be as good as you."

Beau is the kind of kid that always encourages others rather than feed his own ego.

"Of course you will, with practice...and my guidance."

Caleb appreciates the encouragement.

"Right, sure I will. You are the best player in the entire club."

"And you are the best basketball player on our team. I can't hit that stupid basket to save my life."

Now it is Caleb's turn to be encouraging.

"True, but with practice...and MY guidance you can learn."

Beau picks up the soccer ball.

"Good one."

Caleb looks at the trophies on the shelves in Beau's room.

"And then there is lacrosse."

Beau agrees.

"Yep, we are the best!"

They high five.

Looking in a mirror, Myra painstakingly applies lipstick, careful not to go outside the lip lines. Angela watches in wonder.

"Your mom lets you wear lipstick?"

"No. But she isn't here right now, is she?"

Myra stands up. "Have a seat, Angela. Time to do your hair."

Angela takes the seat.

"You are so good at this stuff. I bet you become a famous fashion designer or a model."

Myra begins to tease Angela's hair

"Maybe, but I wish I had your brains."

"You know, we can team up and start a company."

Myra likes the idea but sees a small issue.

"Yeah, that would be great, but we need people to practice on."

Angela thinks for a minute.

"Why don't we practice on our brothers?"

"And just how are we going to convince those two jocks to let us?"

"Simple. We both have dirt on them so we make them a deal. If they let us do it once, we promise not to tell our parents or post it on Facebook."

They look at each other knowing it is a great idea, sure to succeed.

Myra touches Angela's shoulder.

"See? You are the brains!"

Katherine is pouring her heart out to her Sarah, who takes the bottle and pours another triple.

"He is so absorbed in his work that he ignores us. I don't know what has happened to him. When I met him he was so warm and caring. Ambitious, driven, charming--all the things girls growing up think they want."

"Well...he is still...um, you know...um...driven," Sarah says, trying to lighten the mood.

There is a moment of silence. "Wish he was that way in the bedroom."

Realizing what she has just said, Katherine shakes her head, looks at Sarah. They crack up with laughter.

"Oh, sis. You can't mean that."

"I can't mean what I don't remember."

She pours more scotch, missing the glass a little.

"Whoopssss...daddy goin mad us at. I mean, us mad...oh, what the heck. He's goin...ah, let him be pissed."

John and Tom are enjoying a glass of cognac and a fine Cuban cigar. Tom swirls the cognac around in the glass, breaths in the fumes, and takes a tiny sip as John educates him on the liquor.

"This is a Henri IV, Cognac Grande Champagne. It was given to me by a very happy client while I was in the Middle East last month. Believe it or not, it cost two million dollars a bottle."

"I must admit it is beyond delicious." Tom takes another tiny sip.

"You won't get any better than this."

Tom is wondering if this is the right moment to share his idea with John. Not out of fear of it being stolen but more out of fear that John will be condescending and arrogant with regard to the concept. He takes a gulp and waits for the smooth cognac to reach his stomach.

On the drive over Tom had mentioned his idea to Sarah, who thought it was brilliant. When he voiced his concern to her she explained to him that fear will stop anyone from getting what they want. If John shoots the idea down it doesn't mean it's a bad idea, it means he hasn't found the right partner for his project. Sarah suggests that if John does decline, then another opportunity that might prove better for him will come along sooner or later. He must believe in his concept and present it with all the confidence of a plan that has been well thought out. He takes a deep breath and leans toward John.

"I have a business proposition that I am confident you will find interesting and profitable."

"And what would that be?" John replies with a bit of condescension in his tone, just as Tom feared. But now that he has his attention, he doesn't care about John's tone. He just wants to present his concept.

"All right, here is the structure of the deal. We have a software program that…"

John's cell goes off. He looks relieved not to have to listen to Tom.

"Hold on." He looks at the call coming in. "Sorry, Tom, I have to take this. It's the deal out of Israel." He gets up and walks away.

"Of course it is." Tom leans back in his chair, resigned to keeping his business proposal to himself.

Angela and Myra have their hands on their hips as they bend their heads left and right. They stare proudly and intently at what they have created standing in front of them.

"What do you think?" Angela asks.

"I think we did pretty good."

Beau and Caleb are in full makeup with teased wigs. Both wear dresses, painted nails, and high heels. They are not happy.

Beau gives the evil eye to his sister.

"If you breathe a single word of this to anyone, I promise I'll make more trouble for you than you can handle."

She gives him a sweet smirk.

"Don't worry your pretty little head. A deal is a deal."

"And that goes double for you, Myra."

"You two can be so sensitive at times. It's only a little makeup and high heels."

With that, both girls double over in laughter. The boys take off the wigs, toss them on the floor, and begin to wipe off their makeup.

Katherine and Sarah continue their discussion, but the scotch has taken over and they are slurring their words. Katherine's mascara is running from crying. Sarah takes a Kleenex and cleans her up.

Sarah hiccups. "Are you kiidng? He won't bbbbuild the village for the kids?"

Shaking her head left, right, left, right, left, right. "Nupe... I mean nip... nope. That's what I mean, nopey."

"I'm so sorry, sis. Hey, maybe we can blild it for the kids."

"Blild?"

They both laugh. "NOOOOOOOOOOOOOOOOOO. Can't touch the willage without OCD Johnny boy."

"Maybe thhhe kidths could ass him. Ask him." She hiccups again.

"Been there, done that - no good."

"What a selfish...."

Her words are cut short when John enters the kitchen, followed by Tom. He sees the girls are plastered and shakes his head.

"I have to go to the office for a little while."

Katherine is too far gone to make a decent argument but tries anyway.

"It's frickin' Thanksgiving. Give it a whest."

John is not amused. "Thanksgiving is over, and it looks like you could use some... rest."

He turns without saying goodbye and leaves. For a moment all is quiet. Sarah looks at Tom and waves the half-empty bottle at him. Katherine and Sarah look at each other, hysterical laughter erupts.

After what Tom has been through on the porch he is only too ready to join them.

"What the hell. Pour me a double."

Chapter Seven

New York City takes pride in its Christmas decorations. The enormous Christmas tree at Rockefeller Center draws tourists from around the world. Beneath the tree is an ice skating pond filled with skaters at all levels of experience. Some hold each other one arm in front and one arm behind as they skate in synchrony. Watching them takes back many an onlooker to a simpler time when things weren't so complicated and people took time to live their lives to the fullest.

Cartier Jewelers always wraps their building in large ribbons with a huge bow. The Empire State

Building exhibits lights in the colorful Christmas fashion. Saks and Neiman Marcus entice shoppers to stop and gawk at their astonishingly beautiful window displays. Santa Clauses listen as the children on their laps reveal what they want for Christmas and receive the occasional hug. Above many streets hang snowflakes, ornaments, icicles, and Santa in his sleigh pulled by eight reindeer led by Rudolph, with a brightly lit red nose.

The air is filled with the smell of roasting chestnuts and salted pretzels--two of New York's most famous signature street foods. Slices of pizza and hot coffee or hot chocolate keep shoppers on the go, warm, and fueled so they can continue to seek out the best holiday deals. Shoppers pass one another with arms filled with Christmas presents. The Salvation Army stands on many a corner with full brass and choir singing Christmas carols. A sprinkling of snow compels people in the street to bundle up. Scarves are wrapped tightly to keep the chilly air from creeping down warm necks. Smiles and greetings of "Merry Christmas" are in abundance. It is a peaceful and loving time in a typically harried and aggressive city.

The Christmas spirit is alive below John's office window, but he takes no notice, nor does he care to participate. He sits at his desk looking at his father's watch. He tightens his lips, holding back years of pent up emotions--emotions that he will never confront or expose to anyone. They are his personal demons and ones that he has securely caged and safely locked away.

Laura has just finished an impromptu meeting with staff members and has been designated as the one to approach John. She comes into his office and waits for John to look up. He is slightly perturbed that his moment has been shattered.

"What is it, Laura?"

She prepares herself by straightening her dress, standing erect, and clearing her throat. She knows this is a sensitive subject and that broaching it could trigger an angry fit from John.

"The staff was wondering if there is going to be a Christmas party this year."

As suspected, John is not receptive.

"Is that all everyone thinks about? How about I'm wondering if they can concentrate on their jobs?"

Laura doesn't say a word. She returns to her desk, knowing she has failed the staff.

Christmas for Katherine, Angela, and Beau is always exciting. They spend days shopping and looking at the enormous variety offered by the array of stores. In a single file, they descend the escalator followed by Katherine's limo driver, whose arms are filled with wrapped gifts.

Once they reach the bottom and are clear of the crowd exiting the escalator, Katherine addresses her family.

"Anyone feel like some food or something to drink?"

Beau jumps in first. "I'm hungry."

Angela shakes her head.

"You're always hungry. I would love some hot chocolate."

Not to be out done, Beau fires back, "And you always want anything that has chocolate."

Katherine's limo driver looks on with a smile having heard this many times.

Katherine always finds middle ground so that all are satisfied.

"Okay, then it's settled. We eat and then have some hot chocolate."

Her driver knows his cue when he hears it.

"I'll put the packages in the car, Mrs. Daily."

A warm and appreciative smile lights up Katherine's face.

"Thank you, David. Sometimes I don't know what I would do without your help."

"It is my pleasure, Mrs. Daily. I'll see you all back

at the car."

Katherine and the kids head to their favorite spot in the store for food and to enjoy some deliciously thick and rich hot chocolate.

Light pierces through torn curtains, accenting a smoke-filled room. The apartment is a complete mess. Dishes are piled in the sink, empty takeout cartons are scattered around the room. The stench is so strong that even cockroaches shun the place.

Zack, Caucasian male, early thirties, his hair disheveled and dressed in tattered clothing, is pouring two large glasses of liquor. His partner Leon, African American male, early thirties, with dreadlocks that extend down below his shoulders, is equally disheveled and similarly dressed as he paces around the room.

"Man, I hate this time of year," Zack says.

"Why's that?"

"You are dense, aren't you." Zack finishes his drink.

"Bite me - oh yeah, now I get it. Yo mamma didn't get ya nothin fer Christmas and Santa is a drunk."

"Did you have any friends growing up?" Zack asks Leon while he pours another glass and raises his for a toast.

"What should we toast to?" Leon asks.

"To our freedom as of two weeks ago."

They clink glasses. Zack is deep in thought. Then suddenly he jolts.

"Hey, man - I got an idea."

Leon, sensing nothing good is about to come out of Zack's mouth, says, "Last idea you had cost me a year in jail."

"Cute... How's about we go shopping for a Christmas gift?"

"That liquor has gone to your head. We ain't got no dough."

"Exactly - so we get us a nice set of wheels compliments of Santa."

Leon thinks about it then smiles. "Ya know, you're not as dumb as you look."

Having finished a snack and hot chocolate, Katherine and the kids leave the department store. They stop along the way, deciding to pick out a few more Christmas gifts for friends. Beau is humming something.

"Mom, can we sing our favorite Christmas song?"

Angela recognizes the song Beau is humming and is excited to sing along.

"Yeah, please Mom. You know, 'O Holy Night'."

Katherine adores these moments and cherishes the memories they create that will last a lifetime. She is sad that John so rarely shares in these special times with them anymore.

"Okay - Angela, you start."

O Holy Night! The stars are brightly shining.

Beau joins in. *It is the night of the dear Savior's birth.*

The three of them get into the limo and continue the song. They are in perfect harmony, with an imaginary choir and orchestra accompanying them.

Long lay the world in sin and error pining.

David hums as he closes the limo door with the family safely inside, singing their hearts out.

Zack and Leon have scouted out several blocks in search of a car to steal. Zack points to one, but Leon thinks it is too posh. Leon scans the area and sees the perfect set of wheels. He points at it. Leon nods. They approach the car and use a wire coat hanger to unlock it. Zack immediately delves below the dash and starts to hotwire the car while Leon keeps a lookout. Several cars pass without noticing anything suspicious. Leon becomes impatient and starts to pace. He leans on the car.

"What's taking you so long?"

"Almost got it."

The engine roars, and Zack looks up from under the dash.

"Merry Christmas. You drive."

Leon jumps behind the wheel. Zack rides shotgun. The car takes off at full speed, clipping a parked car. Zack lets out a hearty laugh, enjoying the ride like a kid on a roller coaster.

"Nice technique."

Leon joins in with laughter of his own. The car fishtails down the road, knocking into piles of trash along the street.

Inside the limo the singing continues. Their voices warmed up, it is louder now. *Till He appeared and the Spirit felt its worth.*

Zack and Leon's stolen car swerves around a corner and passes a parked police car. The cops look at each other and switch on the lights and siren in hot pursuit.

Zack and Leon pass a bottle back and forth. Leon glances in the rearview mirror when he hears the siren.

"Hey, Zack, look, a lighted Christmas tree is following us."

"Guess we need to see if Santa can keep up." Zack looks in the rearview mirror and laughs. Leon stomps on the gas pedal and leads the cops on a merry chase through the city streets. They swerve into oncoming traffic, barely missing other vehicles. Several cars crash into each other to avoid a head-on collision.

Zack and Leon think this is the funniest thing they have seen since they got thrown into the clink a year earlier. The car veers onto the sidewalk. Pedestrians dive out of the way to avoid being struck down. Garbage cans, tables, and discarded furniture fall victim to their intoxicated recklessness. Their car fishtails into a narrow alley with the police car in hot pursuit.

One of the policemen looks at the computer screen, grabs the microphone, keys it, and speaks over the radio.

"We are in high-speed pursuit of a stolen car heading uptown. We're at 81st and Madison."

Both cars race through the city streets and into another alley. At the other end of the alley, without hesitation and heedless of oncoming traffic, they come flying out, barely missing cars as they drive on both sides of the road. Out of nowhere, a bus heads directly in their path. The bus driver tries to swerve to avoid a collision, but it is no use. The bus hits the car, sending it through the intersection.

Katherine and the kids continue singing O Holy Night...

For yonder breaks a new and glorious morn. FALL ON YOUR KNEES! OH, HEAR THE ANGELS' VOICES!"

SLAM! The limo is violently T-boned by Leon and

Zack's car. Katherine, Beau, and Angela fly through the air, bouncing around inside the limo as it spins out of control. Presents and broken glass swirl in the air as their bodies are slammed around until the limo comes to a violent stop.

The limo, the bus, and the car are mangled into a twisted mess of metal. Presents and broken glass litter the crash site. The pursuing police car is already at the scene and sirens are heard in the distance. A single hub cap spins to a stop.

John is looking at his father's watch when the second hand suddenly stops. Annoyed, he calls to his assistant.

"Laura, I thought you got a new battery for my watch."

Laura enters his office and is visibly upset. John sees her.

"Let me guess, the coffee machine is broken."

She starts to tear up and can barely get the words out of her mouth.

"There's been an accident."

The ER is a beehive of activity. Police, firefighters, EMTs, and ambulance personnel are working at a fever pitch. Nonemergency patients are put off to the side as life-threatening injuries are given first priority. Codes are bellowed out to the attending physicians, who respond immediately. Results of patients' tests come from out-of-breath interns. Doctors are rushed into emergency surgeries followed by support staff and essential equipment.

In the midst of this orchestrated confusion, John rushes in, closely followed by Sarah and Tom.

"My name is John Daily and my family has been brought here. I want to see the head of the hospital now," he tells the nurse at the desk.

The nurse briefly pauses to address John. "I know who you are, Mr. Daily."

"Good. So we can dispense with any pleasantries and get me the head of this hospital."

Immune to John's attempt at intimidation, she responds, "I'll see what I can do."

John's veins pop out on the sides of his neck. He is not used to being treated any other way than with immediacy and with his satisfaction foremost in mind.

"See what you can do? Are you stupid? That wasn't a request!"

Sarah senses the tension. "John, please calm down."

"Calm down? My family has been in an accident and you want me to calm down?"

Sarah understands his frustration but wants him to know that his attitude will get him nowhere in a hospital. She decides today is the day to tell him he needs to listen and not demand. She takes a breath and is about to speak when Dr. Pardee approaches John, Sarah, and Tom.

"Mr. Daily?"

"Yes, I'm Mr. Daily."

The doctor extends his hand. "I'm Dr. Pardee. I am the physician who attended your family. Can we please go into my office to talk."

John shakes the doctor's hand and follows him to his office.

John, Sarah, and Tom take a seat in front of the doctor's desk.

"I want to know the names of the people responsible for this accident."

"I'm afraid that won't do you any good. They were DOA. Mr. Daily, your family's condition is very serious."

"How serious are you talking about?"

"They all are in comas and in critical condition. I am afraid short of a miracle their chances of survival are very low."

Sarah breaks down. Tom holds her. John just stares at the doctor without saying a thing.

"Mr. Daily, I am very sorry. If you like I can prescribe something to help you sleep."

"I want to see them."

"Of course. However, they are currently being prepped for surgery. Once they are out of surgery, I will talk with you again."

John stands up and without a word leaves. Sarah and Tom thank the doctor and request that he keep them informed.

When John arrives home he hesitates getting out of the limo, knowing that he will be entering an empty house. No kids running to greet him, no Katherine smiling and waiting to have dinner with the family. John's limo driver stands by the open door. John looks at him and then at the staff members waiting by the door. He steps out of the limo and tells his driver that he will not need him for the rest of the night and that he will call him when he needs him.

John enters the house and calls the staff together. He informs them of the situation. Several break down in tears and others offer words of reassurance, none of which John wants to see or hear.

"I will not need your services until this situation is cleared up. You'll be compensated during your time off and when my family..." He chokes up for a second then recovers. "Comes home. You will all be informed to return to your normal duties. That is all. Goodnight."

John sees them all out, locks the door, sets the alarm, and stands in the entryway surrounded by a deafening silence. He is paralyzed with doubt that his family will ever come home. After a few moments, he removes his coat, hangs it up in the hallway closet, and heads upstairs.

John walks into his bedroom feeling emotionally drained. He is not used to having these feelings, for that matter he is not used to having any feelings at all. He has long since buried them. Emotions to him are a sign of weakness, and they allow the competition to get the upper hand, something he vowed never to let happen.

He sits on the edge of his bed and picks up a picture of his family. The thought of losing them sears through his mind. He has lost his mom and dad and can't fathom the idea of losing his wife and children.

He slips off the bed and falls on his knees, holding the framed picture. He tries to scream but nothing comes out. The pain is overwhelming. Thoughts of his parents' deaths continue to haunt his mind. He is all alone, with no one to turn to for comfort.

After an hour spent being overwhelmed by raw emotions, he gathers himself up and replaces the picture on the nightstand. He notices an envelope leaning against the table lamp. It is addressed to

Santa. He opens it and reads the letter.

> *Hi Santa, it's me Beau. I have been a good boy this year and would like to have an electric racecar set for Christmas please. Here's my sister. Hi Santa, I have been a good girl so may I please have that pretty doll I saw yesterday when I was shopping with mommy...oh, also - PLEASE can you ask daddy to build the village for us - We miss it.* (Beau again...) *Yeah, that's double for me. Do you still like chocolate chip cookies?*
>
> *Love, Beau and Angela.*

John holds the letter to his chest, stands up, walks over to his liquor cabinet, grabs a bottle of scotch, pours a half glass, downs it in one swallow, and walks out of the bedroom.

He enters a pitch black room and flips a switch. The large basement is tastefully decorated and includes a large movie screen. John pours himself another drink and swallows it without hesitation. He does it again, then he walks over to a large closet door and opens it. Inside are stacks of boxes labeled "Village." He opens one of the boxes and takes out a few of the figurines. He pours another drink and downs it.

"I'm gonna... to... to build the vest billage ever... in the world, or the universe, maybe eben da Nort Pole, and then... so when my family comes..."

He can't bring himself to say any more. He breaths heavily as he proceeds to take out more of the village from the closet.

"Okay, whadda we got here."

He takes several of the boxes over to a table and unpacks them, gently placing the pieces down one at a time. As he continues to pull them out he comes across the one that he talked to as a kid, the one that told John he wanted ice skates for Christmas.

"Hey, Billy, I remember you. I'm a weeee bit fuzzy so help me out here. Did you ever get your skates for ice... I mean ice for ska...ice skates? Well, if I never mentioned it to ya, I got my bicycle. But now I know how Dad, or should I say Santa, afforded it."

He places the figurine down on the table and sits in a chair. He pours another double and downs it. He rocks back and forth in the chair as his vision blurs. His eyelids grow heavy and close and within seconds he is asleep.

In his alcohol-induced state of unconsciousness, John dreams of a time when he ran into the family living room, where his parents would be sitting next to the Christmas tree. John sees his brand new bicycle and runs over to it. He goes up to his mom and kisses her and then does the same with his dad.

John's mom smiles warmly at her son, her heart filled with happiness.

"I guess Santa must have thought you were a really good boy this year."

She glances over at Christopher, her warm smile emanating the warmth of an angel. He smiles at the sight of his son experiencing so much pure joy.

"I am really happy for you, son."

John looks toward the Christmas village and wheels his bike over to the table. He picks up Billy.

"Billy, look - Santa got me a bicycle. Did you get your ice skates?"

He responds as Billy.

"I don't know. We haven't opened our presents yet."

John speaks to him as if he is a real person.

"Remember what we always say...."

John takes the figurine and runs in a circle.

"I BELIEVE...I BELIEVE..."

The night has slipped into the early morning. John is still in the chair, his eyes closed as his lips mumbles. "I... I... believe... I believe."

Chapter Eight

Tom is reading the newspaper and enjoying a cup of coffee as Sarah finishes getting the kids off to school. Outside, the school bus sits idling as the giggling neighborhood kids get onboard waving goodbye and throwing kisses to their mothers. Sarah makes sure Myra and Caleb have their backpacks, she kisses them goodbye, and watches as they climb into the bus.

The bus driver closes the door and heads to his next stop. Once the bus is safely underway, Sarah returns to the kitchen and sits next to Tom. Had Tom looked up from his newspaper and coffee he would have noticed a distressed look on her face. Oblivious to her feelings, he continues reading his newspaper. Sarah waits for a few minutes before saying anything.

"Tom, I am worried about John."

From behind the newspaper he chuckles.

"That's rich. Why would you worry about that--"

"Because he is my sister's husband. Regardless of how he acts."

Tom lowers his paper and sees she is upset.

"Okay, so what's the concern...problem... whatever you want to call it?"

"I called him at his office, and his assistant said he hasn't been there for three days. She got a call from his house staff saying that he let them all go until further notice."

"So are you thinking he did something stupid?"

"I'm not sure what I think. But I want you to go over there and check on him."

"Are you serious?"

"Yes, I am. Please, Tom, for me?"

Tom weighs his options knowing that the wrong response right now could escalate things very quickly, and considering that it has to do with John he feels like it simply wouldn't be worth it.

"What makes you so sure he will even answer the doorbell... or is even capable of answering it?"

"I'm her sister." She shows Tom a house key. "I

have the alarm code, too. Please, Tom, we don't need any more pain in this family."

Tom sees her eyes filling with tears and goes to her.

"If it will make you happy, I will drive over there."

With tears rolling down her cheeks, she falls into his arms.

"You're a good man, Tom."

On the way to John's house, Tom thinks about all the stress John has caused his own family and Tom's family as well. He can't seem to grasp the concept that this man has more money than ninety-nine percent of the people on the planet and still wants more. *Power is a funny thing*, he thinks. It drives people past the point of reasonable thinking and isolates them from reality. When you have that kind of money, nothing has a value anymore. If you want something you simply buy it without suffering any financial consequence. You just open the bill and pay it without hesitation. Tom wonders when—or even if—such a person can understand the concept of *enough*. At what point does a person realize they have more than they will ever need, that their family will be taken care of for generations to come, and that it is time to sit back and enjoy the fruits of their labor. Share some of it with people you love and do some good for humanity. He shakes his head and smiles, knowing John will never have that epiphany, and for that Tom truly feels sorry for him.

Tom maneuvers the long driveway, around the large fountain accenting the front entrance circular drive, and parks. He gets out, walks to the door, and rings the bell. He waits for a while before ringing it again. He jiggles the knob, but the door is locked. He rings the bell a third time. Resigned to the apparent fact that no one will be answering the door, he takes the key out of his pocket and stares at it. He inserts the key into the lock, opens the door, and steps inside. He enters the code turning off the beeping alarm and closes the door behind him.

"Hello, anybody home? John... John, are you here? It's me, Tom."

Tom walks around the main floor but doesn't find anyone. He goes upstairs to the master bedroom and notices the picture and envelope on the undisturbed bed. He takes it as a good sign that John was here at some point. He reads the letter and starts to think that Sarah might have been right to worry about John. Maybe he did do something stupid. There's only one way to find out for sure, and that's to finish searching the house. If John doesn't turn up, then Tom will be forced to call the police and report John as a missing person. Given John's celebrity and notoriety, the police will take immediate action. Tom checks the bathroom and the tub--both empty.

Completing the upstairs sweep, Tom goes back downstairs and continues to look around. Scanning the room, he notices the basement door standing open. He looks down the darkened stairway then descends with trepidation.

"Hello. John? Are you down there?"

Tom thinks that he really doesn't need this. What if he goes down there and finds John dead? What does he tell Sarah? Or better yet, how would he bring himself to tell her anything at all? Would he just leave him and tell her he wasn't home and suggest the police be called and let them find the body? Every scenario leads Tom to the same conclusion. He hopes John is alive so he doesn't have to be the bearer of bad news.

From the foot of the stairs, he scans the room and sees John's arm dangling from a chair and freezes, thinking the worst had come to pass. He hesitates and considers running back up the stairs, getting in his car, driving to work, calling Sarah, and saying he didn't find anything. He knows that would be the safest way out, but his conscience won't let him do it. He stares at John's arm, willing it to move.

"John... John, it's me, Tom. Are you all right?"

John doesn't move. Tom approaches. He circles the chair and to his immense relief finds John breathing, albeit drunk and disheveled

"Well, at least you are alive. John, wake up. John..."

He shakes John a few times. John slowly opens his eyes.

"Tom? Where am I? How long have I been here?"

"You are home and I don't know how long you've been down here, but from the looks of you, I would venture to guess a day or two."

"I look that bad?"

"About eight shots from looking good."

Tom pulls him up to his feet. John wobbles as Tom supports him.

"Let's get you cleaned up."

"Any word about my family?"

Tom hesitates to say anything. John can see it in his eyes.

"Sorry, John - nothing's changed."

Tom takes John upstairs to his bathroom and starts a shower. Once he is sure John is okay, he leaves the bathroom to call Sarah.

"Hi, honey, it's me."

"Did you find him? Is he okay?"

"Yes, I found him. He's a mess but okay."

"Where is he now?"

"I got him in the shower. I'll make sure he is safe, then I have to get to work."

"Thanks, Tom. I love you for doing this. I know he hasn't been pleasant with you over the years, but he is my sister's husband and the kids' uncle."

"I love you, too, and it's fine. I have a thick skin. I should get off to work. I'll call you later. Bye, honey."

He hangs up the phone and, unbeknownst to Tom, John is gulping more scotch in the shower.

Tom calls out, "How you doing, John?"

"I'm good. You don't need to stay, I'll be fine."

Tom is hesitant to leave.

"You sure? I can make you something to eat if you are hungry."

"Not necessary. I'll fix something later. Just lock the door on the way out."

Tom looks toward the shower and whispers to himself, "You're welcome. Thanks for checking in on me, Tom. Give my love to your family." Once a jerk, always a jerk. Tom shakes his head and leaves.

John finishes showering, gets out, grabs a towel, and heads straight to the phone and makes a call.

"Dr. Pardee. It's Mr. Daily calling."

John waits for a short time.

"Hello, Mr. Daily."

"Is there any change with my family's condition?"

"I take it you didn't get my voicemail."

John is a bit embarrassed. "Sorry, Doc. No, I didn't check the messages."

"I'm sorry, Mr. Daily, but their condition has deteriorated a bit."

John sinks onto the corner of the bed.

"Mr. Daily, are you still there?"

"Yeah. Can I see them yet?"

"Yes, of course."

John immediately hangs up the phone and grabs the scotch. The phone rings and he picks it up.

"Hello?"

"Oh my God. Mr. Daily, this is Laura. I have been trying to reach you for days. Are you okay?"

"I'm fine. What can I do for you?"

Laura is taken aback and not sure what to say.

"Are you planning on coming in? What do I tell the staff? They are asking a lot of--"

John loses his patience.

"Tell them to keep working and mind their own business."

John puts down the phone.

On the way to the hospital John is filled with unresolved emotion. He wonders if there are other doctors anywhere in the world he can bring in to help his family. He makes several calls on his cell, but every physician he talks to tells him the same thing; that there is nothing they can help him with. John is distraught and refuses to accept their collective negativity. He calls a friend who puts his faith in alternative medicine, but even his friend sadly reports that there is nothing that can help his family.

John enters the hospital and goes straight to his family's room. Opening the door, he is taken aback by the sight of all the life support machines as well as the bruised condition of his family's bodies. Tears well up as he struggles to maintain his composure. He goes to each one and gently kisses them. He tells them how much he misses them and that he is sure they will be home for Christmas. After kissing Katherine he falls to his knees, wondering why his family is being punished for his selfishness. John's inner strength is dwindling as he gets up and once again kisses each one with the promise of returning to take them home.

Entering his house, John grabs a bottle of scotch and heads to the basement.

He takes out several buildings and more figurines. He gulps from the bottle. He looks at his father's watch. The second hand is still not moving.

"Damn it. I don't even know what time it is."

He takes out a farmhouse and looks at it.

"I remember this house. It always reminded me of our farmhouse."

John turns on a work light, points it at the table, places the farmhouse down gently, and speaks to the villagers.

"Remember when we were all on the farm and the village was in our living room? We had fun, didn't we? Life was easier even though we were so poor."

John is having a hard time standing up. He falls into a chair. He leans over and grabs the bottle and takes a large swig. His eyes are bloodshot and they slowly close.

An unrecognizable voice is heard in the basement. His face twitches at the sound.

"Help... help... please. Help us..."

John stirs in his chair. The voice continues.

"I know you can hear us. We need your help... Why won't you answer us?"

John's eyes open. He looks around the room, unsure of what he is hearing.

"Hello? Who's there? Tom, is that you?"

No one is there.

Again John hears the voice.

"Help... Help us, please... Please answer us."

John looks around the room again but this time

with curiosity. He still sees no one. He gets up and moves to the foot of the stairs and listens, trying to determine if someone is upstairs walking around. He checks the alarm system and finds it armed, with no notification of a breach. He shakes his head to try and clear his thoughts.

"Must have been a dream."

The voice returns.

"I know you can hear us. Please help us. You are our only hope."

John turns in a half-circle, stopping when he thinks he is oriented toward where the voice is coming from. Straight ahead of him is the village. He walks over and looks down. The figurines appear to be moving.

From the viewpoint of the figurines on the table, John is silhouetted against the work light giving him what appears to be a white aura.

A woman's voice calls out. "Look, in the sky. Our prayers have been answered."

"Hello. Are you talking to me?" John is very confused.

"Yes. We have been praying for you to come help us."

A boy's voice chimes in. "Please help us."

More voices join in, asking him to answer their

prayers. John pulls away from the table and shakes his head.

"Great. Now I'm hallucinating."

As he steps away from the path of the light the voices cease. He looks over at the table and the figurines are still. He sits in his chair, utterly confused.

"Not sure what just happened--or even *if* it happened--but... I've got to get out of this basement... I... am... going to move the village to the living room and build the best one ever so that when my family comes..."

He takes another gulp of scotch, closes his eyes, and falls asleep.

Chapter Nine

Daily Investment employees continue to function, but with growing concerns about their future employment. The cooler talk has escalated into a frenzy of speculation. Will they have a job if John's family doesn't make it? And if that happens, what will John be like? Will he be more understanding, more driven, or will he become even more hardened? Some claim to have heard that the family isn't going to recover. Others speculate that the company will fail if John doesn't return soon. There is talk that John has hired people to find out who did this to his family. None realize that the two responsible are already dead.

Laura catches wind of these conversations and quickly approaches each person and squashes the rumors. She is tough, and they will not challenge her knowing she has John's ear. She is always supportive of the staff, but if pushed to choose, she will side with John out of loyalty.

Clients calls in from all over the world concerned about their investments and wanting to know if the company has lost its leadership. Laura manages to keep things relatively calm, reassuring all the investors and business associates that John is active and working from home. She feels badly about lying to their clients, but at the same time she is banking on John's strength to pull him through. If not, she too will be in the unemployment line.

The fresh morning air carries with it the scent of coming snow. The skies are dark and foreboding, threatening to unleash a winter storm. Laura lives only fifteen minutes from the office and enjoys her routine of stopping every morning for coffee with one sugar and a splash of milk, saying hi to Jeff, who is busy behind the corner cart serving hot beverages, bagels with cream cheese, and sharing a happy comment with his customers.

Laura continues down the cold streets, sipping her coffee, lost in thought. Christmas shoppers are already in full swing, the city sports the merriest of decorations, and yet she feels empty, scared, and lonely at the thought of what John and his family are going through. Despite being tough as nails, John has always taken care of her. He has a soft spot for Laura regardless of his outward insensitivity. Her emotions swell the closer she gets to the office, where she will have to check her emotions at the door and function as the professional that John has come to rely on. As she approaches the entrance to the building she is greeted by Father Theo.

"Hi, Laura," Father Theo says with a warm smile.

"Hello, Father Theo. What brings you here?" she says, trying to keep her emotions at bay.

He is holding a piece of paper, which he hands to her.

"I was wondering if you could give this to Mr. Daily. It is a letter to Santa Claus written by the children in the orphanage. His help could make many children very happy this Christmas. Would you please give this to..."

He sees that she is upset.

"I'm sorry, child, I did not mean to upset you."

"It's not that, Father. I guess you don't know, but Mr. Daily's family was in a serious car accident and they probably will not live. He is beside himself and hasn't been to the office in days."

"I am deeply sorry for this. I will pray for them. I am sure his heart must be very heavy."

Father Theo walks away as Laura stares at the letter. She looks after Father Theo, tosses her empty coffee cup into the nearby trashcan, and enters the building.

The hospital never stops bustling with nurses, doctors, and patients. All of a sudden a loud signal goes off in one of the monitors.

A nurse bellows with authority, "Code Blue, ICU - Room #119."

Another nurse jumps into action, picking up the intercom. "Stat - Room #119, cardiac arrhythmia."

Doctor Pardee along with several nurses rushes through the door, followed by a defibrillator and support staff. The nameplate of the doors reads, 'Daily'. Angela is lying on the bed shaking. The team rushes in and starts to treat her. Doctor Pardee takes charge.

"Give me the paddles at 300."

A nurse hands him the paddles. He places them on Angela's chest.

"Clear."

Doctor Pardee releases the charge. Angela's body arches.

John is drunk and sound asleep in a chair when suddenly his body jolts simultaneously as Angela does in the hospital. He remains asleep, lingering in a dream.

Seven-year-old John is back on his family's farm, playing with figurines from the Christmas village.

"Billy, I don't know what to do."

He responds as Billy.

"You mean about your dad?"

"Yeah, he is really sad about mom. He says we will have to sell our farm animals because we need money. I guess we really are poor."

"Are you sad?" Billy asks.

"I miss my mom more than anything. Billy, if I was rich I could have saved her life. I don't care what it takes, but one day I'll be very rich, then I'll have anything I want and my dad will never be poor again."

John speaks as several villagers.

"Can you help find me a job?"

"Our house is cold and we have no heat."

"My son needs an operation and we have no money."

John picks up one figurine after another, listening to their plight. He examines the beggar.

"And how did your life come to this? Did that mean old Mr. Scrooge do this to you?"

John puts down the figurine gingerly and draws a deep breath.

"Okay, villagers, listen up. I, John Daily, will grow up to be very rich and powerful, then I will give you all what you want no matter what it takes. No one will go hungry... or be without a job... or be in need of anything. Nothing and no one will stand in my way. And no one will be mean to anyone. You have my promise."

A second jolt rockets through John's body. His eyes open as he grabs his chest. He gets out of the chair and shakes it off. He is no longer in the basement. He has moved the village to the living room. All the curtains are closed and the rest of the room is in darkness. The work lights are turned on and directed toward the village table.

The platform is completely built and about half of the village has been constructed. The village now includes mountains, buildings, figurines, and trees, similar to the ones from his childhood but more detailed and with updated Dickens porcelain houses. Next to the table remains a pile of unopened boxes containing additional village pieces. John steps back as a thought strikes him.

"Oh my God. I remember now...all the promises to the people of the village. I promised to help them when

I got powerful and wealthy... Wait, what am I saying? Promises to figurines?" He starts to laugh. "Now I know I have lost it."

He walks around the darkened room, and from the platform he hears the voice of a boy calling out.

"Are you there? Can you hear me?"

John walks over and stands in front of the work light and looks down into the village. The figurines are moving again. This time he indulges himself.

"Yes, I'm here. Can you hear me?"

Viewed from inside the village, the same aura of light surrounds John's head. John hears his reply, but it is from the figurine Billy.

"Yes, we can hear your voice from the sky. We have prayed very hard to be heard, and now you are answering our prayers."

The other people of the village gather and look toward the sky. They all witness the silhouette of John.

A priest crosses himself. "It's a miracle."

A woman on her knees implores, "We knew in our hearts you would not forget us."

The other villagers fall to their knees and bow their heads. Billy looks at his mother with a smile.

"See, mom, I told you... All you have to do is BELIEVE."

John looks on with memories of happy times spent as a child flooding his heart. He can feel the presence of his mom and dad, wishing all the while that they were there with him to enjoy Christmas and his mom's homemade chocolate chip cookies. It is a bittersweet moment. His feelings seep into his heart with the profound weight of emotional stress because his parents are no longer alive. Overwhelmed, tears start to stream down his face. As they drip and fall toward the village, the tears slow down in time and transform into snow. The villagers look up.

"Snow... Snow... It's a sign from heaven."

Billy rises from his knees with the widest smile his face can accommodate. He starts to run in a circle around the villagers with his hands held out, looking toward the sky and screaming out loud, "I believe... I BELIEVE... I BELIEVE!"

Fully exhausted and emotionally drained, John falls back in his chair, grabs the picture of his family, and holds it close to his chest.

He looks at the photograph, and whispers, "I believe... I believe... I believe."

Holding onto the picture for dear life, John falls asleep.

The night is a restless one for John. His mind is the battleground for conflicted dreams of childhood and all his business adventures in a struggle for his soul. Nightmarish visions haunt his thoughts. An empty house with no wife and kids, going to work with no purpose, becoming more dependent on alcohol, abandoning all ties with Sarah and Tom and their family, sitting alone in the darkness eating TV dinners, growing thin from lack of nutrition, thoughts of suicide, no friends, his businesses failing because he no longer cares, and the house slipping into disrepair around him.

John wakes up in a sweat, having seen what the future would be without his family. Unable to process his feelings, he gulps more scotch in hopes of dulling the pain and silencing the inner turmoil. His entire body is convulsing as the fabric of his life unwinds. No Katherine, no kids, no life--this would be his ultimate nightmare. But still he doesn't realize that he has created this himself. He is in denial thinking that all his efforts have been made on behalf of his family. The unconfronted truth is that John never forgave himself for the death of his mother. Had he been older he would have made the money needed to get her the operation and she would still be alive. It is a moment in time where he made a promise to the people of the village and to himself to never be poor again. Even after he had achieved vast riches he would be confronted with another emotional trauma; the death of his father. Although in no way his fault, he blames himself for both deaths. It never occurs to John that money and power can't fix everything. Some things are beyond human control.

Early the next morning, a delivery van pulls up to the house. Weighed down by boxes labeled 'Racing car set' and 'Princess doll' he is barely able to ring the doorbell. John opens the door. He is unshaven, his eyes bloodshot, and wearing the same clothes from the night before. The delivery man can smell the liquor on John. He eyes him with concern.

"Good morning, Mr. Daily. I, um... need your signature for this delivery. Looks like some lucky boy and girl are getting some nice presents for Christmas."

Without looking up, John takes the pad and signs it. The delivery man hands over the packages, which John places inside the house. The delivery man turns to leave and pauses.

With his back to John he says, "Mr. Daily..." continuing as he turns around, "are you..."

By the time he turns around John is inside his house closing the door. The lock is engaged.

"...all right?"

The delivery man stands there for a moment, contemplating what to do. Knowing who John is and how the Daily's demand privacy, he walks away.

Inside the house John leans his back against the front door exhausted and dehydrated. The phone rings. John can only stare at the boxes, knowing how beautifully Katherine would have wrapped them before placing them underneath the Christmas tree. John and Katherine would lie in wait, eager to behold their children's smiles when they discovered they got exactly what they asked Santa for—it was one of the enjoyable moments he felt as a child. Nothing can come close to the memory of that moment, a memory that John has neglected to capture for many years. He always relies on Katherine to do the shopping, including gifts for herself, because he was too tied up at the office. The phone continues ringing. John finally hears it and answers in a weak voice.

"Hello."

"Hello, Mr. Daily?"

"Yes, this is he."

"Um... Mr. Daily, this is Dr. Pardee. You need to come to the hospital today to discuss your family."

John forces himself to focus without asking about the nature of the meeting.

"I'll be right there."

John hangs up and catches his reflection in the mirror. He looks himself up and down and goes upstairs to get ready. While shaving he imagines the day that lies before him, one filled with good news of restoring his life the way it was before the accident. A long-lost smile comes to him as he anticipates the family being home for Christmas and their surprise when they see the village in their living room in all its glory.

John's limo pulls up in front of the hospital. The driver opens the door and John steps out, clean shaven and dressed in a suit.

"Please wait. I will be back as soon as I can."

"Yes, sir," replies his driver.

John walks to the front door of the hospital.

John's driver shakes his head. "I think that is the first time I ever heard him say please. Poor bastard."

John enters the hospital and goes directly to Dr. Pardee's office and is immediately greeted by the doctor's assistant. She walks John into the office, offers him a beverage, which John declines, and tells him the doctor will join him shortly. John takes a seat and looks through some magazines. Each minute feels like an eternity as he is unaccustomed to waiting on anything. A few minutes later the doctor comes in and takes a seat behind his desk.

John is on edge from lack of sleep and nutrition. He cuts to the chase.

"I assume you have good news, doctor?"

"I'm afraid not, Mr. Daily."

John is taken aback, suddenly fearing the worst. He stares at the doctor waiting for him to say something.

"Mr. Daily, your daughter had a cardiac arrhythmia."

John grips the arm of the chair, thinking he is about to be told that Angela died. His heart starts to race with anxiety and shooting pains. He musters enough strength to pose the question.

"Is she..." But he can't finish the sentence.

"No, but it was very close. We were able to resuscitate and stabilize her, but in the last 24 hours I haven't seen the type of improvement I was hoping for. And unfortunately that goes for your son and wife as well."

The doctor looks down at his desk, not sure how to proceed.

"Is there something else, doctor?"

"Mr. Daily, I would like you to consider signing these."

He hands John some papers. John takes a few seconds to read them and gets out of his chair and paces the room. He looks at the doctor then back at the papers. John starts to get mad.

"You want me to sign papers so you can farm my family for their organs!"

"Mr. Daily, I would not frame it that way."

"Really. Then how would you frame asking me to sign donor papers?"

"Precautionary."

"Precautionary!"

Doctor Pardee tries to deescalate the situation before it gets out of hand and he loses the opportunity to save other people's lives.

"I assure you Mr. Daily, we are doing everything possible. But if anything goes wrong, we will have very little time to act on this. I know this is not easy to digest--and I am not saying we are at that point yet-- but their conditions are not improving and we have an obligation to potential recipients to inquire."

John is extremely confused and has no idea what to do or say.

"Why don't you take the papers home and think about it. I will call you tomorrow to discuss this further."

John turns and walks out of Dr. Pardee's office, holding the papers by his side. Aimlessly he makes his way to the ICU, where his family lies with machines hooked up to each of them to sustain their lives. John leans against the glass wall looking in. He raises his hands to his head. In one hand are the papers from the doctor.

"Katherine, Beau, Angela, I miss you so much. Please come home... I... am so sorry for..."

His face contorts with anguish. He crumbles the donor papers.

"Kids... I'm building the village. You should see it. It is the best one ever. Please come home... I can't do this without you..."

After a few minutes, John's self-preservation mode kicks in. He has never given up on anything. He is the type of person that, once he makes up his mind, there is no stopping him from getting what he wants. He gathers himself and straightens out his clothes.

"I'm not giving up on you. I believe... I believe... I believe with all my heart you will come home." He closes his eyes. "I believe..."

John lets the donor papers fall to the floor landing at his feet. He turns to leave, stepping on them as he walks away.

The ride home is somber, and his driver does not utter a word, having long since come to know when John needs his quiet time. The limo enters the property and pulls up to the house. John gets out.

"Will there be anything else this evening, Mr. Daily?"

"No. If I need you I will give you a call."

"Mr. Daily, would you like me to get some dinner for you?"

John looks at his driver and sees the compassion in his eyes. He shakes his head.

"I'm not really hungry. Go home and be with your family. I'll be fine. Goodnight, Charles.

John goes into the house and closes the door.

"I'll be a son of a gun. I didn't think he even knew my name. Maybe there is hope for you after all."

Charles gets in the limo. He pulls away from the house and heads home.

John closes the door and turns on a light. He is beside himself with grief and tries desperately to hold it together. He grabs a bottle of liquor and gulps down several long drinks. In mid gulp, he walks into the living room and turns on the work lights. He stares at the village for a while, then sits on the portion of the unfinished village platform and lets out a tortured cry.

"WHY? WHY THEM AND NOT ME? Mom... Dad..."

In desperation he looks up. "God... if you can hear me... please... help me... I don't want to live without them."

He curls up into a fetal position. Then his body springs open, his arms and legs flailing as he screams.

"Katherine, Angela, Beau, please be strong and

fight to come home! I'm sorry for not being there for you more... Please forgive me!"

John's demeanor softens for the first time since he left Dr. Pardee's office.

"I would do anything to make things right... Anything."

He falls onto his back and curls back into a fetal position, staring up at the work light. The light seems to smudge as John's vision becomes blurred. His eyes are bloodshot and unable to focus. The work light becomes brighter and brighter until his entire body is engulfed in the white light. He slips into unconsciousness, lying on the village platform, all alone in his empty mansion.

Chapter Ten

Voices and sounds of the city filter into John's ears. Christmas carolers are singing while horse-drawn carriages, trailing laughter, fade in the distance. A Santa laughs a hearty "Ho-ho-ho..."

John is unsure of where the sounds are coming from or whether he is asleep or awake. His head throbs from the alcohol and his mouth is dry from lack of water. John's eyes open and the bright white light fades. He sits up and looks around. To his left are his work lights, standing tall and appearing out of scale. He looks all around to discover that the ground is covered in white felt--the same kind of white felt that covers the unfinished village platform. Convinced he is dreaming, he stands up and turns around and is at once mesmerized and confused. There, before him, is the village he has been building, except now he is a part of it. John shakes his head trying to clear it.

"I've got to be dreaming. This is impossible."

He bends down and touches the ground. *This must be a dream.* John rubs his eyes, but the village images do not go away. John can see the edge of the platform and his living room furnishings. He touches his face and feels the sensation. He begins to entertain the notion that he is not dreaming. But if he isn't dreaming, then that can mean only one thing; he really is inside the village. His curiosity takes over and he starts to walk toward the entrance to the village.

People are bustling around gleefully. Everyone is dressed in true Dickens fashion. A group of people look over and notice John entering the town, silhouetted by the work light, from the darkness they call the Outer Boundary. Once John is fully inside the village, the crowd gathers around him in amazement.

"Look, our prayers have been answered. The angel from heaven has come," a village woman exclaims.

From within the crowd a little boy, previously known to John as the figurine of Billy, pokes his head out.

"I hope he brought my ice skates," he says with a grin.

John is swept deeper into the village by the crowd. The people touch him, some kneel in prayer, others kiss his hand and thank him.

"Are you here to help us?

"Will you answer our prayers?"

"I need a job."

"My son needs an operation and I can't afford it."

"The bank is going to take away our home unless we pay the mortgage."

John becomes overwhelmed and runs away. Unsure of what is happening, he ducks into a dark alley and hides behind some cardboard boxes. He sees an old furniture pad and covers his head with it. The villagers walk past the alley looking for John, but he is safely tucked away.

For the moment John thinks he has eluded the crowd and can now start to get his head around his strange situation. A hand taps John's head.

"Hey, mister, they are gone. You're safe now."

John remains still and says nothing. The hand reaches in and taps him on the head again.

"I said it's safe to come out."

John lowers the furniture pad and looks toward the voice. A bum's face comes out of the shadows.

John gets nervous and inches away from the stranger. The bum sees the fright on John's face.

"Relax. You are safe here."

He reaches into his jacket pocket. John looks around for an avenue of escape but sees none. He tenses up. The bum withdraws a sandwich and offers it to John.

"Are you hungry?"

John relaxes. He looks at the sandwich then at the bum.

"Why would you offer me your sandwich?"

"Well, for one thing, I've never seen you in town... and I know everybody here. For another, you seem to be running from that crowd, and you look like you could use some food and a friend."

"A friend? I don't know you."

"On the street there is an unspoken code that people help each other. We don't have much, so in order to survive we share what we got."

The village bum extends his hand, offering the sandwich. John reluctantly takes it. He smells it and takes a bite.

With his mouth full, he says, "I didn't realize how hungry I am."

"Yeah, that happens when the stomach hasn't seen anything for a while. Eventually you stop hurting inside... then you slowly fade to nothing until all the pain stops and you no longer even need food."

John swallows so he can explain himself.

"You misunderstand. I have more money than you can imagine. I eat at the finest restaurants in the world."

The village bum smiles.

"Of course you do. And you probably have a mansion with servants."

"Yes, as a matter of fact..."

"...as a matter of fact we all start to wish for those things, but the only thing we really have is each other and our faith... and that is what gets us by day to day. I pray that one day I will have a job to feed myself and a warm place to rest my head."

John finishes his sandwich.

"I don't understand how you can have faith when you live in the street like this."

"That's just it."

"What's just it?" asks John.

"Faith, my friend."

John leaves the dark alley and cautiously walks along the street, peeking into some of the stores while trying to avoid being recognized by those who saw him enter the village. He passes a volunteer ringing a bell.

"Good day, sir. Can you help the orphans have a

good Christmas this year?"

"Sorry, no."

John stands there, waiting for his head to clear.

The volunteer takes an interest in John.

"Are you okay, sir?"

John clears his throat.

"Yes... I just... well, you see..."

"Are you hungry?"

"Hungry? No, no, I'm fine. Say, does everyone in this town help each other?"

"No, not everyone. There are people that have everything and still want more. Then there are those with little and can't give enough."

John lowers his eyes, shakes his head, and walks away. He walks across the street and into the town park. A young woman is sitting on a bench, crying, as her husband tries to comfort her. "I can't keep pretending. Without this operation our boy is going to die."

"I will find a way to pay for--"

"How? It is going to cost thousands of dollars, and we barely have enough to make ends meet."

"Maybe I can go see--"

"You've tried that and he flatly refused you. He is heartless."

They both look up and see John staring at them.

He looks away. The husband approaches John.

"Are you the angel that came from the outer boundary? Will you please help us in our time of need?"

"I'm sorry, but... you have me mixed up with someone else."

John scurries away, and the man rejoins his wife. John walks down another street and stops short of the bank. The banker, Mr. Bailey, wearing proper English banker attire, and a woman, Mrs. Farland, dressed in her best Sunday clothing that nevertheless reveals years of wear and tear, comes out of the bank.

"I told you inside, Mrs. Farland, that I am late for an appointment and there is nothing I can do."

"Nothing you can do? What kind of a man are you? It is a week before Christmas and you want to evict us from our home? We have been paying the mortgage for the last 20 years without a problem."

"That may be so, but there is a problem now. You are three months behind and Mr.--"

"Don't even mention that man's name."

She softens her approach to him.

"Look, Mr. Bailey, can't you find it in your heart to give us a few months? My husband is looking for a job, but there just isn't any work right now. It will change soon and..."

"We are running a bank, not a charity." He steps closer to her. "I wish there were something I could do, but if I help you then I risk losing my job."

He reaches into his pocket and hands her some money. John notices this and furls his eyebrows.

"Here, this should see you through a week or two."

Understanding the situation, she reluctantly accepts his offer with an expression of hopelessness.

"I will only accept this as a loan, not a handout."

"Okay, that's fine. Now go home and take care of your family. I will make some calls and see if I can help find your husband a job. But that must stay between us, okay?"

"Okay--and thank you."

Mr. Bailey walks away, leaving Mrs. Farland in tears. John stands there watching. He takes a step toward her then stops, suddenly wondering if this is what happened to his mom and dad with the farm. Hearing his own thought, his head turns toward where his thoughts now lie.

"The farm..."

John walks through the village and notices how many of the things are in the exact place where he set them on the platform. He passes the rare book store, the bank, the cobbler, the tavern, the church, and some houses snuggled amongst larger trees that stand in front of mountains reaching for the sky.

John reaches the edge of town and heads toward the farm. He can already imagine what the surroundings will look like. He knows there will be a frozen stream spanned by a cross-bridge with dangling icicles, farm animals moving snow aside to get to the grass below, deer wandering around free and safe, and the tractor parked by the barn covered in snow. Piles of hay will be inside the barn, ready to sustain the animals when the snow is too deep for grazing.

Along the way he passes a lake that is surrounded by the buildings he has carefully placed. The dock sits perfectly secured in the water while a fisherman unloads lobsters. The multiple trees he positioned are all lined up perfectly. Arriving at the road leading up to the farm, he stops to take it all in. Still believing this to be a realistic dream, John walks up the dirt road to the front door of the house and knocks. No answer. He tries the doorknob. It is unlocked.

"Hello? Is anybody home?"

Stepping inside he stops and does a 360-degree turn.

"This is impossible. This is my mom and dad's farmhouse where I grew up. I don't understand... How is this... Why... What is..."

John walks into the kitchen. He lovingly touches

the stove, wishing he could see his mom baking her delicious cookies and preparing a glass of fresh milk direct from one of their cows waiting for him to devour.

John enters the living room where his childhood village was always placed during the Christmas season.

"This is where Dad and I used to build the village while mom made her delicious cookies. I can almost smell them... and remember..."

"Those simple days. Boy, do I miss you, Mom and Dad."

He glances at his dad's watch. The second hand is still. He manages a smile.

"Hey, Dad, I have your watch. You didn't have to sell it for my bike--I would have understood."

He looks again at the watch in hopes the second hand will begin moving. It remains still.

"You both sacrificed so much so that I could have a happy childhood."

John turns around and sees the bicycle that he got that Christmas.

"No way. My bike?"

He smiles as he gingerly brushes his fingertips along the metal.

"Looks as good as the day I got it."

John looks over his shoulder.

"I wonder if my bedroom looks the same."

John opens his door and flicks on the switch to his night lamp. Standing in the doorway, he looks around.

"Unbelievable. It is exactly as I remember it."

John picks up various pieces of memorabilia from his childhood. He goes to the window, sits where he did as a child, and sees the last light of day as the sun sets. A full moon lights up the farm. As he stares out the window, he sniffs something in the air.

"Cookies?"

From behind him John hears a familiar voice.

"Hello, John."

He turns around. Framed in the doorway are his mother and father.

"Mom? Dad? How..."

He runs to them and they all embrace.

"How is this possible? Am I dreaming?"

Christopher puts his hand on his son's shoulder.

"No, son, you are not dreaming. We have been given permission to visit with you for a short time."

"Your dad and I know about your family's accident."

"Mom, are they going to die? I'm lost without them."

"That's up to you."

"Me? But I have no say in their recovery."

His dad gives him a soft but knowing look.

"You'd be surprised by how much you are involved in their recovery. Unfortunately we can't give you the answer. It must come from within. You have to discover it for yourself."

Mary gives John a hint.

"Think about all the things you have seen since you arrived."

"But what can I do here? I have no money, no power, nothing."

His dad smiles, knowing John will eventually find a way out of his dilemma.

"And that is the start of the discovery."

"Think about what you did that brought you here, about who you are inside."

His dad reminds him about something important. "Do you remember the promise you made to your village friends?"

John looks down at the floor then back at his parents.

"I do. I, John Daily, will become very rich and powerful, then I will give you all what you want no matter what it takes."

"I know you will find the answers and do the right thing," his dad says with affirmation.

John's mom looks into his eyes.

"Sometimes answers come in ways we don't expect. Only when a person keeps themselves open do they really hear the answers to their prayers."

"How will I know when I have done that?"

Christopher glances at his old watch on John's wrist.

"Sometimes things stop for a reason."

John looks at his father's watch.

"...and they begin again when it is done from the heart."

"If that is true, then why didn't Father James lend you and mom money when you asked?"

Mary explains. "John, when we asked for help, Father James had to tell us that his church was on the brink of bankruptcy. Otherwise he would have gladly given us the help we asked him for. You need to let go of the past and find forgiveness in your heart."

A bright light starts to form around John's parents. Mary looks up then turns her gaze back to John.

"It is time for us to go, John. We love you more than anything in the whole wide world."

Christopher gives him a hug and a kiss.

"Take care of yourself, my boy. We are very proud of you."

John hugs his mom goodbye then steps back. Their figures start to become transparent as the light engulfs them. Before they disappear, John reaches out toward their fading figures.

"Mom, Dad... I love you... Goodbye."

A light shines through the window. John turns and walks over to it and looks outside. The light dims to a sky now filled with clouds. A single snowflake lands on the window, then another and another.

"Snow!" A childlike smile sweeps across his face.

Chapter Eleven

Daniel, the owner, has spent seventy years working in the rare book store in the town square. He is dressed casually in a sweater vest. Glasses hang on his chest so he can always find them. The door opens with the sound of an old fashioned bell ringing. John enters and see books stacked floor to ceiling. A wooden ladder on a rail stands in the middle of the bookshelves.

John approaches the shop owner. "Good morning."

"Top of the morning to you, sir. Care for a cup of tea?"

"No, thank you."

"Are you looking for a specific book or just browsing?"

"Actually I am doing a little of both. Do you have a book on the origin of this village?"

Daniel looks at him with curiosity. "I do. What is your interest in this village? Are you a writer?"

"No. I am looking for an answer I haven't been able to find anywhere else."

"I see. And you feel it might be found in the origin of this village? I am very interested in what your question might be about."

"I'm not really sure. I just thought maybe if I knew the origin, it might give me a glimpse of the answer or at the least a direction for me to follow."

Daniel climbs two steps on the ladder and pulls a book off the shelf. He comes down and blows the dust from its cover.

"Ah. Here it is. The origin of our village."

"Great. I'll take it."

John reaches into one pocket then the other while Daniel looks on. John looks at Daniel, realizing he doesn't have any money to pay for the book.

"Sorry. It seems I left my wallet at home. I'll come back later to get the book."

John turns to leave.

Daniel stops him from exiting the store.

"No need. Please, take the book. Have you considered going to the church for some guidance?"

John sighs.

"I see. Not a church-goer. Well, sometimes in moments of confusion and doubt, a quiet place might help to sort through feelings."

John looks curiously at Daniel.

"Why are you willing to trust a complete stranger? How do you know I will return?"

"I don't. What I do know is that if that book is that important to you, then I hope the answer to your question and pain can be revealed."

"I... I... um... don't know what to say... Um, thank you, thank you very much."

Daniel nods his head in acknowledgment. John turns and walks out of the shop.

The street is alive with people shopping for Christmas. The large Christmas tree sitting in the middle of the village is almost fully decorated. The final decorations are being placed around the branches to the accompaniment of carolers and vendors offering hot chocolate.

John crosses the street and goes over to a bench, sits, and readies himself to read the book and hopefully find an answer to a question he is not sure is the right one. He opens the cover but is distracted by a loud discussion. An old man is yelling at someone.

"You're late."

"It is only one minute past the hour, sir," pleads someone who is obviously an employee.

John looks across the street but can't see the faces of the men arguing as the old man continues to rant.

"I don't care if it is one second after. I'm not paying you for time you miss. Do you understand?"

Resigned, the employee knows better than to continue with an argument that will certainly lead to him losing his job, something he can't afford right before Christmas.

"Yes, sir."

"Now get to work or you can start looking for another job," barks the old man.

The worker quickly enters the building. The old man follows him inside, closing the door firmly behind him.

John's mind is conflicted, thinking on the one hand that the old man was right about the relationship between an employee and employer while on the other hand feeling something he hasn't felt in a long time; sympathy. John's thoughts are interrupted by a married couple passing by, talking about what just happened.

"Does he ever stop?" the woman asks her husband.

"He is a lonely, miserable old man. Money and power seem to be the only things that are important to him."

She shakes her head in disdain.

"It is a shame he never got married. Maybe a loving family would have made a difference."

John looks down, the stinging words hitting home.

"And even that is not a guarantee." He turns back to the book and starts to read.

> *No one is sure of the exact date of the origin of the village. It is said that one day an angel appeared in the sky and the townspeople began to pray to the angel. As they prayed, miracles began to occur. One morning the villagers woke to find many fully grown trees in and around the village. The town's large Christmas tree was beautifully decorated. To this day no one knows who was responsible or how it happened. The people of the village saw this as a miracle and never questioned their gift. Somehow the town started to expand into the outer*

boundary. The place where the park is now located was once part of that dark place. The villagers went to bed one night and woke up to find the new park. They noticed that the boundary had shrunk. All the villagers prayed for more miracles. Then one day they heard a voice from the sky promising that all their needs would be taken care of. For some unknown reason, the village was plunged into darkness for many long years until recently, when the light returned and an angel came to the village from the outer boundary.

John's head shoots up.

"What? How could this part even have been written yet?"

John closes the book and rushes back into the book store.

Daniel sees John and smiles. "Back so soon?"

John is out of breath and can barely get the words out.

"This book... when was it written and by whom?"

Daniel cocks his head.

"Well, the author is unknown and the book was written back in the 1800s. Why do you ask?"

John opens the book to the first page and hands it to Daniel.

"Please read this out loud."

"Of course, by all means."

> *The village was modeled after a man named Charles Dickens, born in 1812. Dickens was known all over the world for his remarkable characters, his masterful prose he scribed in telling their stories, and his descriptions of the social classes, morals, and values of his time. Some considered him a spokesman for the poor, the downtrodden, and the have-nots because he brought awareness to their plight. Dickens was quoted as saying, "Whether I shall turn out to be the hero of my own life, or whether that station will be held by anybody else, these pages must show."*

John cuts him off and looks at him like he is crazy.

"May I see the book, please?"

Daniel hands him the book. The words are exactly what Daniel just read. Deciding that he just might be losing his mind and that none of this is real, John hands the book back to Daniel.

"Are you all right, sir?"

"I'm not sure anymore."

John leaves the store and walks around aimlessly, lost in thought. He passes a queue of people. As he nears the front of the line a hand reaches out and stops him. It is the bum he met when he first got to the village.

"Hey, friend, remember me?"

John replies, "Yes, yes I do. You shared your sandwich with me. Why are you standing in this line?"

"It's a food bank that the church does for us. Here, get in line with me."

John looks at all the faces of those in line. Instead of seeing sadness he sees peaceful faces filled with hope and joy.

"Won't these other people object to me cutting in line?"

"Heavens no. Everyone knows they will get something to eat. No one goes without a meal."

"Is life that simple for all these people?"

"Well, now it is, but there was a time when they had things. Unfortunately most folks lost a lot, if not all, to a certain greedy so and so. If you catch my meaning."

"And that's okay?"

"No, not at all. But sitting around feeling sorry for yourself won't change a thing. Only the meek..."

John finishes the sentence "...shall inherit the earth."

"Exactly! We believe that someday that greedy man will learn a lesson and give back the things he took from us. Then we can all live in peace and goodwill."

"Thank you. You have given me a clue to what I need to do. Take care."

"Aren't you hungry?"

"Yes, hungry to save what's left of my life."

John walks along the line until he reaches the front, where he sees a priest and volunteers serving food. He recalls his promise to the people of the village. But how is he going to manage it without money or power?

Chapter Twelve

The air wafting from the freshly frozen lake mixes with the smell of smoke from fireplaces in the neighboring homes. A vendor sells hot chocolate to skaters seeking to keep warm. Other skaters are enjoying the frozen lake in an ice dance that is reminiscent of old Hollywood movies. Flowing scarves keep the skaters' necks warm with each pass across the ice. A man is ice fishing. The Blue Star Ice Company loads large blocks of ice onto trucks for deliveries. The doors of the Grapes Inn open and close with patrons coming and going--satisfied customers with bellies filled with perfectly prepared food. Other patrons retire to their rooms for a nap before the night activities begin. There are several cottages surrounding the lake with people tending to their snow-covered paths, chopping wood for their stoves, and chasing after children to don their mittens before playing. A couple rides by on horses. A passing sled is filled with people singing. Kids throw snowballs from behind snow-clad forts. The atmosphere is one of fun and good humor. John finds an empty bench by the lake and sits. He takes in all the activities and for a brief moment forgets his troubles. Taking a deep breath, he looks toward the sky.

"I don't know where to begin or why you would even listen to me, but..."

Children run past John laughing and throwing snowballs. One accidentally hits him.

"Sorry, mister. I didn't mean to hit you."

John smiles at the child and his friends, who are waiting to see what John does.

"It's all right. You go have fun with your friends."

"Thank you, sir. God bless you. And Merry Christmas."

The kids run off. John looks up again.

"Why are you punishing my family for the things I have done wrong?" John stares at the sky in search of an answer. "Show me a sign. Show me the way. Help me help these people. What can I do to right my wrongs? My mom said sometimes answers come in ways we don't expect. That only when a person keeps themselves open do they really hear the answers to their prayers. So my prayer is to please help me to be open to hearing the answers. I'm lost and I need help."

John buries his head in his hands. A gust of wind swirls around him. As it passes, he hears someone clearing their throat. Opening his eyes, he sees Billy on his knees in front of him.

"Sorry if I am interrupting, but I have been looking for you since you came from heaven. Did you have to go back to heaven for a while?"

"Billy, I didn't come from heaven. I am not an angel. Please get off your knees."

Billy stands up. John signals for him to sit down next to him.

"You see, Billy, right now I am looking for answers to my own prayers. So why would I be doing that if I came from heaven?"

He thinks for a minute then snaps his fingers.

"Because angels have to help people before they get their wings."

John sees Billy's naive innocence and decides not to go any farther.

"You know, Billy, you are a very smart kid. How

did you get so smart?"

Proudly he answers, "It comes from my dad. He says that once I understand any problem, then it no longer is a problem. It becomes a fun challenge to find the answer."

"Sounds like you have one smart dad."

"Yeah, he is the greatest. So will I get my ice skates this year for Christmas?"

John smiles from ear to ear. In actually talking to the "real" Billy he is starting to feel things he hasn't felt in a long time. Childhood feelings of giving and hope sneak into hairline breaches in the hardened shell he has developed over the years. It was the lack of money that made their lives tough living on the farm, and now money lessons once again are rearing their ugly heads. This time, money is abundant but no less tough on forfeits... except the forfeits are affecting his family in a different way than when he was poor. Being poor or being rich both come with a dark side that entails emptiness, loneliness, isolation, and frustration.

He smiles at Billy. "You bet you'll get those ice skates."

Billy jumps up and down then runs in a circle. "YEAH! THANKS!" Billy looks at his watch. "Whoops. If it is okay with you, I have to go home now to have dinner."

"See you later, Billy."

As Billy starts to leave John calls out to him.

"Billy!"

He turns to John.

"Thank you... I really mean it, thank you."

"My pleasure, Mr. Angel."

"Billy, would you mind if I walk you home?"

"I'd like that."

Billy can't help asking John about something that all people want to know.

"What is heaven like?"

John laughs, knowing he is about to say what his own father would have said to him if he asked such a question.

"What do you think it is like, Billy?"

John and Billy head toward town. Billy reaches up and takes John's hand. John is touched by Billy's gesture of friendship and closes his hand around Billy's. In a way they have been friends since childhood, except John has grown up while Billy, as a village figurine, remains innocent to life's hardships. John knows there is something good in the air, but just what that is isn't exactly clear to him yet. Walking with Billy is a dream come true. His lifelong imaginary friend only wants ice skates for Christmas, and John is now determined to make sure his Christmas wish comes true for real.

Chapter Thirteen

Emotionally and physically drained, John stands by the entrance to the village looking out over the empty space that he knows is the unfinished portion. Countless thoughts race through his mind seeking a solution for the people of the village and his own life struggles. He is used to being in control and calling the shots and now feels like a fish out of water. He has always been the master of his environment, with no one questioning his actions or request. What John wants, John gets. It is the promise he made to the people of the village and to himself when he was a small boy. He has accomplished his goal of becoming rich and powerful, but at what expense? And how does that help him now? He knows the answer is out there if he can just find the right question or at least a sign to follow. John walks back into the village. Villagers rush to him with pleas for help.

"Look, he's back... Where did you go? We thought you left us... Will you help us?"

John is surrounded, with no way to escape. He sees hope in their faces and relaxes.

"I want to help you, but... I am not sure how to do that."

Billy steps out from behind the crowd.

"Hello, Mr. Angel."

"Hi, Billy."

"Mr. Angel, can I ask you a question?"

"Sure, Billy."

"Before you were an angel, what were you? What did you do in life?"

"Well, Billy, I am... I was a businessman and had many companies."

"How did you do all that?"

"I... um... started with nothing, and saw an opportunity, which led to another one, and slowly over time I built an empire of wealth and power because I learned how to negotiate really well. I never took no for an answer."

"Did you help people or were you mean?"

John knows the answer to Billy's question but does not want to say it. A welcome distraction comes from a short distance away when an all too familiar scene unfolds and causes a commotion across the village square.

"I don't care if Christmas is coming. You do your work."

"Yes, sir. But I was wondering if I could have tonight off since it is Christmas Eve?"

"Christmas Eve is as bad as Christmas. Isn't it enough I have to pay for you to not work on Christmas Day? Now before you get fired, go inside and get to work. Bah, Humbug."

"Yes sir, Mr. Scrooge."

John's head spins around, and a thought begins to percolates.

"Scrooge?"

The villagers explain to John who he is.

"Sour old man."

"No one likes him."

"He is unreasonable."

"Hates Christmas."

"No one can talk to him."

"He forces us to pay high mortgages so he can take away our homes and land."

"Never gives a dime to charity."

"Still owns the first penny he made."

"The man is scared of his own shadow."

John smiles when he hears that Scrooge is scared of his own shadow. Bells go off in John's negotiating mind, and a plot develops to help the villagers and perhaps himself. After all, John knows how that story ends. John turns back to the villagers.

"I think I might have the answer to all your prayers."

John walks across the street and over to the building where Scrooge works. Entering the building, John encounters a cold, dimly lit, smoke-filled office with only a single employee. The place reeks of unpleasantness. John walks over to the worker, who is shocked to see anyone voluntarily entering the office.

"May I help you?"

"Yes. I would like to see Mr. Scrooge."

"Do you have an appointment?" says the worker mechanically.

"No. Just tell Mr. Scrooge I have a business proposition for him."

The worker looks toward the door to Scrooge's office and then back to John.

"Are you the angel we all saw?" he whispers. "If so, if he fires me, will you help me get another job?"

John leans in so the worker will feel safe having a conversation with him.

"Trust me, he isn't going to fire you... As a matter of fact, tomorrow he will be a completely different man."

The worker looks at John, then turns and goes into Scrooge's office. A minute passes and John hears some loud discussion. The worker returns to John.

"You can go in, but he is not in a good mood."

"Thanks."

John walks into Scrooge's office and closes the door. Without a single word, Scrooge gestures for him to have a seat. Scrooge eyes him up and down, trying to decide what to do with this brassy fellow who dares to come to him with a proposition.

"So, you are the supposed angel who came from the Outer Boundary that everyone keeps yakking about? What do you want with me?"

"I have a business proposal for you."

"And what might that be? Wings to get into heaven? I don't believe in that childish dribble."

"What if I told you that you will be visited by three ghosts tonight that will show you your life from the past, present, and the future?"

"I'd say you were as crazy as everyone else in this pathetic town."

John continues his tactics.

"Fair enough. I'll make you a deal. If you're visited tonight by the three ghosts that I speak of, then you agree to grant everyone in this town their wishes. You will give back their properties, free and clear, pay for needed operations, set up a charity that generates enough interest income to feed every person in town, make sure that everyone has a job, and take care of all the orphan's needs."

Scrooge notices John touching his watch.

"That is quite a proposal. I have a counterproposal for you."

John looks at Scrooge with distrust.

"I'm listening."

"If these ghosts of yours don't visit me tonight... then you work for me for free for the rest of your life."

John is taken aback. "That's a steep proposal."

"So is giving those worthless people back what is rightfully mine. They don't deserve such generosity. Do we have a deal or not?"

John adjusts the watch as he thinks about it.

"We have a deal."

Scrooge has him where he wants him, and his greed takes over.

"That's not all."

John looks at him dumbfounded.

"Meaning?"

"You will not only work for me for the rest of your life, but you will live on barely enough to keep you poor. No comforts at all."

"And you wonder why people don't like you?"

"Bah, humbug. I don't give a rat's ass about them. And I don't care what their problems are. I run many businesses."

John hears his own venomous words flung back at him. He now knows what he sounded like to so many loyal employees and friends.

"Mr. Scrooge, I have used those same words, and I now regret it. You and I have a lot in common."

Not impressed, Scrooge goes for the jugular.

"You've wasted enough of my time with ghost stories and proposals. If you don't want to accept the terms of my offer then get out of my office."

John reaches out his hand.

"Deal."

Scrooge takes his hand to shake it, but suddenly turns John's wrist over.

"One last thing."

"What else could you ask for?"

"Your watch."

John withdraws his hand. His father's watch is one of the few things John cannot risk losing. He knows if he says no then Scrooge will kill the deal. John has been checkmated for the first time in his life. His head spins with potential ways to negotiate out of giving up his dad's watch, but it always ends with Scrooge throwing him out of his office.

Scrooge looks into John's eyes with a piercing resolve of having won the negotiation.

"Well?"

Reluctantly John hands the watch to Scrooge.

Scrooge takes the watch and examines it.

"You'll have to sign an agreement in front of the magistrate binding you to this arrangement."

"Where do I sign?"

Chapter Fourteen

John is standing outside looking up at Scrooge's bedroom. His anxiety level is high. He paces while talking out loud. He knows if this plan doesn't work, he will be an indentured slave to the stingiest man of all time. John wants more than anything to return home and find out the fate of his family. He has set in motion the fulfillment of all his childhood promises to the people of the village and the final moment of truth is at hand. What if the ghosts don't appear? *How will I ever get out and make things right?* he thinks. *Will anyone ever know where I am?* He looks up at Scrooge's window, secure in knowing the classic story of the Christmas ghosts will come to pass. But what could be taking so long?

"Come on, ghosts, don't let me down."

As time passes John starts to lose hope. Maybe the story is only a story about the ghosts, and since he is in a make-believe village, then perhaps Scrooge will not be visited that night or any other night.

He closes his eyes and concentrates, trying to come up with some options. Try as he might, nothing comes to mind that will free him from his agreement with Scrooge. He is locked into a deal that is predicated on a story and not on reality.

He then thinks about what his mother and father told him when they came to visit. He is sure he has done everything possible to make this right. John's energy fades and his head lowers as he anticipates the sense of desperation he faces. He raises his head one last time to see if anything is happening in Scrooge's bedroom. As his eyes settle on Scrooge's bedroom window, lights flicker on and off. Shadows loom on the walls. He hears Scrooge's scream of fear. John falls to his knees and looks up at the sky

"Mom, Dad, thank you for helping me find myself. I have been so foolish with all that I have... I ignored my family when they should be the most important thing in the world. Forgive me for... No, I need to forgive myself and make things right."

John stares into the night sky.

"I swear, if I am given another chance, I will do the right thing... I... I believe... I believe with all my heart."

John folds his hands in prayer and is silently forgiving himself for his thoughtlessness when his father's watch materializes on his wrist. The star's light grows brighter until John is totally engulfed in the light and cannot see anything. He closes his eyes.

As it dissipates, his eyes remain tightly closed. He feels the light fade and his eyes flicker open. He is on his back in the same fetal position as when he fell asleep, before he journeyed inside the Christmas village. He sits up and looks around. He is on the village platform in his living room. He shakes his head, trying to clear his mind. Out of habit, he glances at his watch. The second hand is still not moving. He gets off the platform and heads directly to the phone and makes a call. He taps his fingers, waiting for the call to be answered. It finally is picked up and John doesn't hesitate.

"Hello?"

"Hello, Mr. Daily?" a voice replies.

"Yes."

John takes a deep breath and says nothing.

"Mr. Daily, are you still there?"

"Yes, doctor."

"I'm not sure how to say this, but..."

John closes his eyes, expecting to hear the worst.

"Well... if you believe in such a thing... a miracle has happened. Your family has come out of their comas, and I think they will have a full recovery. I just can't explain it."

John smiles and spins in a circle, tangling himself in the phone cord.

"Can I pick them up?"

"We need two days for observation and to run further tests to make sure all is fine. At that point, assuming everything checks out, they can be released to go home."

"Thank you, doctor. Thank you! God bless you and Merry Christmas."

"Don't thank me. I had nothing to do with this... And Merry Christmas to you, too, Mr. Daily."

"Please call me John. By the way, what day is it?"

"It's Thursday, December 22nd."

"Great! There's still time to make a few changes."

Confused, Dr. Pardee says, "I don't understand what that means."

"It means I can right some wrongs. Goodbye, Doc. See you in two days."

John hangs up and calls Laura.

"Hello, Mr. Daily's office."

"Hi, Laura, it's John."

"Mr. Daily?"

"Call me John, Laura."

Laura is shocked and at a loss for words.

"Okay. Are you all right?"

He responds with a chuckle, "I couldn't be better. Please call my house staff and have them return. In two days, my family is coming home."

Laura sheds happy tears.

"Mr. Daily... I mean John... how is... Never mind, that is great news."

"Please tell the staff that I am on my way in to the office after I shave and shower. You can tell them that we will be closed from December 23rd through January 2nd. With pay."

"I am sure that will make them all very happy, but wouldn't you like to tell them the good news?"

"No, Laura, you always deliver. the bad news. It's time you give them something positive. I'm going to stop by the hospital. Oh, and tell them to expect a bonus, and raises as well."

John hangs up. He smiles and stretches his arms out and begins to run in a circle.

"I did it. I BELIEVE. Mom, Dad, I did it. I did it, I did it. I hope you can see me and are proud... I have my family back and they are alive and well! I will never forget again! I BELIEVE."

Chapter Fifteen

John arrives at his office, clean shaven and dressed in something casual. He enters the building followed by workers carrying a large Christmas tree.

"Please set it up here."

John walks over to the guard, who is prepared to incur more abuse.

"Would you please turn on some Christmas music and change that TV station to something festive."

The guard's defensive posture turns into a smile from ear to ear.

"Yes sir, Mr. Daily."

John goes up to his office in the public elevator

with other workers. They are not sure what to make of him being in there with them. John offers them the season's greetings and asks how their families are doing and what they plan to do over the Christmas vacation. They are unsure at the idea of a Christmas vacation, but no one challenges the gift. The elevator doors open and the waiting employees see John and take a step backwards. John greets them with smiles and cheers, passing them by on his way to the conference room.

John stands in front of the staff with Ralph and Yamachi on a teleconference.

"How are we doing and why are you both there?"

Ralph answers first. "I am sorry to say that the numbers will require 3-6 more weeks."

Yamachi chimes in next. "I, uh, sorry but similar results."

John steps closer to the teleconference screen.

"Gentlemen, it is going to be Christmas soon. You need to be home with your families."

They are speechless.

"Laura, please arrange for Ralph and Yamachi to be on the next flight home... and make the reservation in first class."

He turns to the staff.

"As for all of you... Merry Christmas! I will see you

all next year."

John goes around shaking hands and eventually approaches Laura and gives her a hug.

"You have put up with a lot... and I am sorry. Now go home and enjoy Christmas with your family."

"Merry Christmas, John."

She gives him a kiss on the cheek. He returns it.

"Merry Christmas, Laura."

John's limo drives slowly along the city streets. He sees the bum he beat up standing on the sidewalk and asks his driver to pull over. John gets out of the limo.

"You! Did you come to kick my ass again? Christmas present?"

"No, I am here to offer you a job."

"Yeah, right."

John walks over to him and points at the limo, gesturing for him to get in.

"If you will forgive me for my stupidity and allow me to make it right, I would be very grateful."

The bum hesitates, but then realizes that John is sincere. He gets in the car.

The day continues to unfold with John walking into the orphanage where Father Theo serves. He is followed by several men carrying large bags filled with presents for the children.

"Hello, Father Theo."

"Hello, John. What's all this?"

"A miracle, Father. A miracle."

Father Theo smiles. John takes out the list that Father Theo gave to Laura. John also hands him a check.

"I believe everything on your list is here."

Father Theo glances at the check and does a double take.

"John... a million dollars?"

"More to come, Father. Merry Christmas."

"Merry Christmas to you, John, and God bless you."

"He already has, Father. He already has."

John's next stop is Tom and Sarah's house. John talks with Tom while Sarah listens intently.

"I want to see your business proposal after the first of the year. Let's come up with a game plan to implement it."

"Don't you want to know what it is?" asks Tom.

"No, Tom. I trust you wouldn't present anything that you weren't convinced was viable."

Sarah looks at Tom then walks over to John and hugs him.

"Thank you, John. This means the world to Tom and me."

"I am looking forward to us spending more time as

a family... if that is okay with you?"

With tears in her eyes she says, "Of course it is."

Tom is overjoyed and glad to be able to talk with John without having to cope with his condescending attitude.

"I'd like that very much, John."

John's final stop is the hospital. John sits on Katherine's bed. He strokes her hand lovingly. Her finger twitches, then her hand slowly closes around his. John looks down at Katherine's hand. He notices that the second hand on his dad's watch starts to tick again. Katherine's eyes open.

"John?"

"Katherine? Oh, Katherine, I was so scared."

He holds her and kisses her.

Angela's eyes open and she sees him. "Daddy?"

Beau's eyes open. "Hi, Daddy."

He hugs each of them.

"Hi, Beau. How are you feeling?"

"Good."

"Hi, sweetheart. I missed you."

"Daddy, I had a very strange dream. I dreamt that a small boy was playing with our village. And there were voices asking him for help."

John stands up, a curious look on his face.

"I wasn't going to say anything, but I also had a

dream that Dad was talking to Scrooge. Oh and I also smelled cookies," says Beau.

They all look at Katherine.

"Yeah, me, too. I had a dream that you were with your mom and dad. It was very emotional but was..."

John finishes her sentence.

"Comforting. I guess dreams can come true... if you believe."

John goes back to Katherine and takes her hand.

"I thought I was going to lose you all. It was horrible."

"Well, you didn't, thank God. John, more than anything I want us all to go home."

"Once the doctor gives the okay we'll do just that, and we'll celebrate the most wonderful Christmas ever. I love you, Katherine."

"I love you, too."

They kiss. Angela looks at Beau, who scrunches his face as if to say "Eww, cooties."

The limo arrives at their home. , John's driver opens the doors and John, Katherine, Angela, and Beau get out. The entire staff greets them as they enter the house. Inside, the remaining staff are lined up, obscuring the village behind them. John addresses them.

"I am very happy that you all came back to help

welcome my family home. Thank you. It has been a very difficult time, to say the least. I want you all to know that I have included a Christmas present in each of your paychecks. Now it is time for all of you to go home to your families and enjoy Christmas."

One by one the staff members thank John and welcome the family home. As they leave, Beau glances over and sees the village. A smile spreads across his face from ear to ear. Beau nudges Angela and then shoots his gaze toward the living room. She sees the most magnificent village they have ever had.

"Daddy... you built the village!"

Katherine looks at John with overwhelming love in her eyes. He goes over and holds her in his arms.

"I thought I was going to lose you all. Please forgive me for being so blind. I am so sorry for..."

"Ssshhhh... I love you, too."

Angela and Beau are busy pointing out different things they spot in the village.

"WOW! Look at this..."

"No, look at this..."

They continue to revel in their enjoyment of the village. John and Katherine join them. Angela grows quiet and stares at something in the village. Beau looks at what she is staring at. John and Katherine look at each other.

"Is there something wrong, kids? Did I make a mistake?" asks John.

Angela points to something.

"No, Daddy. I just don't remember seeing that figurine before."

"Yeah, me neither," agrees Beau.

John leans over. "Which one?"

Both kids reply, "That one."

John looks into the village. There in the middle of the frozen lake is Billy with his arms outstretched, scarf blowing in the wind, and a huge smile on his face, skating on his brand new ice skates.

END

ABOUT THE AUTHOR

John Callas is a veteran writer/director/producer in the entertainment business. His experience ranges from the worldwide release of feature films to numerous motion picture trailers, national and international commercials, live action title sequences, laser disc projects, a documentary shot on location in Russia, as well as having been the Worldwide VP for The Walt Disney Company while working at a large post production facility. John wrote and directed the feature film *No Solicitors* starring Eric Roberts and has adapted NY Times bestselling author, William H. LaBarge's book, *Lightning Strikes Twice*. John is also a published author of: *Secrets, When The Rain Stops, No Solicitors, and First Time Parents Survival Guide To Unnecessary And Wild Spending.*

John's prowess can be seen on live action teasers for *Ransom, Dennis The Menace, Body Of Evidence, The Golden Child, Spaceballs, The Glass Menagerie, Cocoon II, Poltergeist III, Betrayed, My Girl, Glenngarry Glenn Ross,* As Well As Title Sequences *For The Two Jakes and A Few Good Men* and a promotional film for an amusement ride from Showscan. John also directed an award-winning short film *The White Gorilla.*

While creating live action teasers for feature films, John had the opportunity to work with notable actors including Mel Gibson, Walter Matthau, Jack Nicholson, Madonna, Eddie Murphy and Mel Brooks.
In addition to working on feature film teasers, his work can be seen in projects for HBO, The Disney Channel, Show Time, the Broadway Play *Phantom Of The Opera* and the 1993 redesigned TRISTAR LOGO.

John's extensive background also includes over 200 commercials for such clients as Kellogg's, Dodge, Sunkist, Sprite, Toyota, Fuji, Volkswagen, Honda, McDonalds, Mazda, Minolta, Jedi Merchandising, Kraft, Jordache, Sea World,

Givenchy and Sonassage with celebrity George Burns and industrial projects for Corporations including Vidal Sassoon, Salomon North America, Nissan and The Kao Corporation Of Japan.

His television experience includes directing a 14-week series entitled *Potentials*, with guests Buckminster Fuller, Norman Cousins, Ray Bradbury, Gene Roddenberry, Timothy Leary and others. He also directed 80 segments for *Bobby's World*, which has been rated the #1 show on Fox 11 Television in its time slot; garnering John an Emmy nomination.

A multi-faceted filmmaker, John's work can be seen in music videos for Glenn Frey Of The Eagles, Bill Wyman Of The Rolling Stones, Jefferson Starship, Sammy Hagar, Rick Springfield, Doobie Brothers, Styx and more.

John has been recognized with: An EMMY nomination for *Bobby's World*, THE NEW YORK CRITICS CHOICE AWARD for *Lone Wolf*, BEST FEATURE at Fright Night Festival, BEST DIRECTOR at Scar A Con festival for *No Solicitors* and several awards for his short *The White Gorilla*, A CLIO and BELDING for his work on the *Sunkist* campaign, BEST OF THE WEST for directorial work on a one-woman show, and an MTV AWARD FOR BEST CONCEPT for Glen Frey's *Smuggler's Blues*.

John holds a Master Degree from Occidental College, and is a member of The Directors Guild Of America.

He lives in Santa Monica, California with his wife Linda, has two sons, Stephan and Nicholas, and their dog, Bandit.

67941073R00109

Made in the USA
San Bernardino, CA
29 January 2018